RANGER PURPOSE

TEXAS RANGER HEROES

LYNN SHANNON

RANGER PURPOSE

God is our refuge and strength, an ever-present help in trouble.

Psalm 46:1

ONE

She needed to be strong and fast to get her baby back.

Ellie Brooks planted her hands on her hips and watched several silver-headed ladies coo over one-year-old Owen. Her foster son grinned, flashing an adorable bottom tooth. One arm held fast to his trusted stuffed dog, Scout, as he used his other hand to grip the edge of a chair for balance. Ellie had left her little man in the care of his "grandmothers" while she helped set up tables and booths for the church bazaar. For the last hour and a half, he'd been cuddled, kissed, and entertained by the Silver Creek sewing circle. Judging from the half-done quilt tossed to the side, Owen's babysitters hadn't completed a stitch since his arrival. It wouldn't be easy to extract him.

"Come on, Owen." Marta Perez clapped her hands and held them out to the little boy. She leaned forward eagerly, her flowing skirt brushing the reception hall floor. "Take a step. You can do it."

Ellie held her breath as Owen let go of the chair. His brow furrowed in concentration. For half a heartbeat, she thought he'd take his first step, but then he landed on the ground, his bottom cushioned by his diaper.

The elderly ladies cooed again, as if he'd done magic. Marta scooped him up with a quickness that defied her seventy-seven years and cuddled him. "You're so cute, I could just eat you up."

Ellie smiled as she approached, sliding the strap of her diaper bag higher on her shoulder. "Careful, Marta. If you start nibbling on him, you'll have to explain it to Child Protective Services."

Marta grinned, completely unbothered. Warm brown eyes peered at her over tortoiseshell glasses. "Let them come. I'd tell them he needed more spoiling."

"Mm-hmm." Ellie extended her arms. "As much as he's loving the attention, it's past his bedtime. If I don't get him home soon, he's going to turn into a pumpkin. A very cranky one."

Marta pouted, kissing the top of Owen's blond curls. "You hear that, mijo? Mama says it's time to go. We don't like it, do we?"

Owen gave a half-hearted whimper, then yawned before sticking his thumb in his mouth.

"That's what I thought." Ellie reached for him, and Marta reluctantly handed him over. Owen immediately rested his head on Ellie's shoulder. A rush of love flooded her, and she patted his back gently while addressing Marta. "Thanks for watching him."

"Anytime, mamasita," Marta said, brushing imaginary lint off his onesie. "He's no trouble at all."

Ellie laughed. "I wouldn't go that far, but he makes up for it in sweetness."

Marta chuckled. "He sure does." She kissed his chubby hand. "Bye, Owen. Be good for your mama."

Ellie waved to the other ladies, adjusted her hold on Owen—he seemed to get heavier with each day—and headed for the exit. Most of the setup for tomorrow's bazaar was finished, but a few locals lingered, chatting about town gossip and goings-on. Many stopped Ellie to pat Owen on the head or remark on how much he'd grown. The entire town of Silver Creek seemed to have adopted the little boy as one of their own from the moment Ellie brought him home from the hospital as a sickly infant. He'd been born premature and with a congenital heart defect. But Owen was a fighter. Love, constant care, and one open-heart surgery later, and he was nearly indistinguishable from any other healthy one-year-old.

Chief of Police Roy O'Neal spotted them coming and held open the heavy door for Ellie. "That's a boy with a fan club." He gently knuckled Owen under the chin. "Keep charming 'em, kid. You'll have this whole county in your pocket by the time you're in kindergarten."

Ellie snorted. "Kindergarten? He won't need nearly that long."

Roy chuckled. "Probably right. Night, Miss Brooks. Drive safe."

"Thanks, Chief."

She stepped out into the balmy spring air. After all this time, the outpouring of love from the townsfolk still caught her off guard. Ellie wasn't a local. She'd only moved to Silver Creek three years ago seeking a fresh start, choosing the town solely because her maternal grandparents had grown up here. She hadn't even known if she would stay.

But memories ran long in this slice of the Texas Hill Country. Ellie had been welcomed with all the enthusiasm of a long-lost relative. At a time when she'd felt alone and deeply discouraged, this town—and the people in it—had saved her, bit by bit. A kind word at the grocery store. A friendly hand repairing her house. An invitation to lunch after church. She made friends. Built a life. Healed. And after a lot of prayer and soul-searching, applied to become a foster mother. Ellie figured it would take ages for a child to be placed with her. She was single, after all.

And then... she'd gotten a phone call about Owen.

Nothing could have prepared Ellie for the monumental sense of responsibility or the overwhelming love she'd felt for the tiny bundle they placed in her arms. Nor had she been prepared for the outpouring of love from the community in the days, weeks, and months that followed.

"Everyone adores you, little man." Ellie kissed Owen's temple. His mouth worked overtime on his thumb, and he gripped Scout tight. He was definitely sleepy. "Did Mrs. Marta and the others wear you out?

We can skip bath time tonight." He'd already had dinner. A bottle and a story were probably all he could manage before a meltdown began.

Ellie picked up her pace. A whisper of wind brushed across her face and tugged at her ponytail, carrying the scent of freshly cut grass. It was still cool enough to be comfortable, but in a few short weeks, summer would arrive. Late May to mid-October could be brutally hot. She wasn't looking forward to it.

The parking lot stood mostly empty, her SUV tucked under a fluorescent light next to an oversized truck. She sighed. The vehicle prevented her from loading Owen on the driver's side, so she circled around to the passenger rear door. A van straddled the dividing white line, taking up two spaces. At least it was far enough away that she could maneuver.

The diaper bag slid to her elbow as she struggled to open the car door. A muscle along her stomach pulled, and the familiar ache courtesy of the bullet wound she'd taken to the gut flared. She ignored the old injury and set Owen down on the floorboard so she could toss the diaper bag into the car. He hated being strapped in, and she braced herself for the upcoming fight.

"Let's get you into your car seat, sweetie." Ellie smoothed one of his runaway curls and gave the sleepy boy a smile. She was just about to launch into a rendition of Mary Had a Little Lamb when the faint scuff of a boot against the pavement reached her ears.

Her attention snapped toward the sound, and she inhaled sharply. A figure in a black mask appeared alongside her bumper. Ellie froze. Her mind couldn't quite accept what her eyes were seeing. It was like a nightmare had materialized out of thin air.

Time slowed as the masked man's gaze went past her, locking onto Owen. Ellie couldn't see his facial features, but she felt his malice straight to her bone marrow. A fear unlike anything she'd ever experienced—and she'd been through some terrifying moments in her life—catapulted her heart into overdrive. She reached for Owen, but then she saw the second masked man closing in from the front of her vehicle.

He came fast and hard, grabbing her shoulders and yanking her back. His grip was rough enough to snap her instincts and her old training into action.

Ellie jabbed him in the stomach. Once. Twice. The movement was practiced, designed to loosen his hold, but her focus was divided. The other masked man was already lifting a wailing Owen out of the vehicle.

He was kidnapping him!

Raw fury and a mother's protective instinct sent fresh adrenaline coursing through her. Ellie rammed her head backward, catching the man holding her under the chin. His grip loosened, and she pivoted hard, breaking his hold. Her arm came up and she struck fast, the heel of her palm ramming into the bridge of his nose. It gave way with a crunch.

He screamed, staggering away as blood gushed down the front of his mask.

Ellie spun. "Owen!"

The other attacker had him in his arms. Poor Owen

thrashed wildly, his terrified screams piercing the night air.

No one was taking her baby.

She launched herself across the space, driving a kick into the kidnapper's kneecap. It buckled beneath him with a crack. He dropped sideways, and before he hit the pavement, she snatched Owen from his arms. The baby's weight was a welcome relief, but there was no time to savor it. Mr. Broken Nose was recovering quickly. He staggered to his feet, rage evident in his stance, and snapped open a collapsible baton with practiced ease. One strike, and she'd likely be on the ground.

Her mind raced through options in a split second. They were boxed in by the two men on either side, her SUV, and the van. There was only one escape route.

Ellie lunged for the SUV's still-open door. Tumbling into the backseat, she yanked the door closed and slammed the lock down. Owen clung to her shirt, still crying. Her hands shook as she shoved the diaper bag out of the way and tucked him under the seat, shielding him with her body.

Her phone. She needed her phone if there was any chance of surviving this.

Ellie's shaking fingers fumbled with the device as she yanked it from her back pocket. She dialed the police chief. Her voice was tight and urgent when he picked up. "Roy, two men are attacking me in the parking lot. They're trying to kidnap Owen—"

Glass shattered.

The side window exploded into a rain of shards as

the baton slammed through it. The man's shadow loomed across the front seat.

Ellie turned, shielding her baby with her body, and whispered a prayer through clenched teeth.

"God, please help us."

TWO

Not his case. Not his problem. And yet, here he was.

Texas Ranger Daniel Perez settled his tan cowboy hat on his head. The church parking lot teemed with official vehicles from the Silver Creek Police Department and the Kendall County Sheriff's Department. Townsfolk lined the west side of the parking lot, held back by deputies and yellow crime scene tape. A familiar voice hollered his name. He turned to find his mother waving from the corner of the parking lot. She stood surrounded by a gaggle of silver-haired ladies, all of whom he'd known his whole life. One of the many perks of growing up in a small town.

"Thank goodness you're here." Marta hugged him tight when he bent to kiss her cheek. The familiar scent of her lavender perfume momentarily carried him back to his childhood. "Ellie needs you. Someone tried to kidnap her baby!"

Ellie Brooks. He'd never met her, but he'd heard

plenty during his weekly phone calls with his mother. Marta had taken the new mom under her wing. Not surprising. She'd never met a stranger in her life and, despite having a slew of grandkids, never tired of adding one more to the pack of chaos.

"I can't imagine why anyone would kidnap a child." Marta pressed her hands to her cheeks. Tears filmed her dark brown eyes. "And from a church parking lot. It's too horrible for words."

The ladies behind her clucked their agreement. Virginia Winters, one of Marta's oldest friends, wrapped an arm around her shoulders in silent comfort. Daniel envied their innocence. He could list dozens of reasons someone might kidnap a child, a grim knowledge gained from nearly two decades in law enforcement. Sometimes, he felt far older than his 49 years.

"You'll help Ellie, won't you?" Virginia demanded. "These criminals need to be found and put into prison."

Every one of the ladies nodded in firm agreement. Their fury and determination were palpable. Daniel feared they might breach the yellow crime scene tape and organize a manhunt of their own—armed with purses, casserole dishes, and a list of suspects alphabetized by maiden name.

He'd learned long ago never to underestimate the power of Silver Creek's matriarchs. These were the women who arranged marriages, revived church budgets, and pulled off fundraisers with military-grade precision. Catching criminals wasn't in their usual repertoire, but he wouldn't put it past them to try. That's why he chose his next words carefully.

"I'll offer my assistance, but ultimately, this case is Chief O'Neal's." Texas Rangers operated mostly as support for local law enforcement. Only in rare exceptions could they take over a case. Most of the time they had to be asked. Daniel motioned behind him. "He has the support of the sheriff's department and may well have everything in hand."

Virginia waved away his words. "This is an all-hands-on-deck situation. If Roy gives you a lick of grief about taking on the case, you send him our way."

Daniel shuddered, thinking of the earful these ladies would give the police chief. He had little doubt Roy could handle it—the man could simply turn off his hearing aid—but still... "Let's not get out the pitchforks quite yet, ladies. Let me assess the situation first." He patted his mom reassuringly on the arm. Her blouse was thin, and the temperature was dropping by the second as the last rays of sunlight faded. "Y'all go on home now. I may be awhile."

The group broke up as Daniel turned to cross the parking lot. He flashed his badge and gave his name to the officer keeping record before ducking under a second string of crime scene tape. Roy stood near the shattered rear window of a silver Hyundai Tucson, a deep frown marring his features. Seventy and reed thin, he'd worked for the police department since Daniel was a child. He'd taken over as chief nearly two decades ago and showed no sign of wanting to retire anytime soon.

"Chief O'Neal." Daniel extended his hand as he approached.

Roy blinked, as if being pulled from deep thoughts, and his crinkled face broke into a grin. "Daniel Perez, it's been far too long, boy. Where have you been hiding yourself?" Roy took Daniel's extended hand and pulled him close for a manly hug. Then he stepped back. "You don't visit us in Silver Creek no more?"

"My apologies, sir. I pop in for family events but never have enough time off to stay for an extended vacation."

Roy chuckled. "Suppose it takes days just to visit your family."

Daniel laughed and nodded. "That it does." He had six brothers and sisters, dozens of aunts and uncles, and too many cousins to count. "They keep getting married and multiplying on me."

That earned him another hearty laugh and a slap on the back. "Your mother is a matchmaker extraordinaire. How you've stayed single so long, I'll never understand."

It was by firm choice. Daniel didn't want to think about his disastrous marriage or the divorce that followed three short years later. He'd been young. And very stupid. Now, he was older and wise enough to know that marriage and kids were not for him. Besides, being single allowed Daniel to focus on his career, which brought him purpose and fulfillment.

He gestured to the shattered window of the SUV. "My mom said there was a kidnapping attempt. She was worried and insisted I come. Sorry to drop in on you out of the blue like this, Chief."

"Not at all. I'm happy to have the help of the Texas Rangers. Probably would've called you myself in the morning." He lifted his cowboy hat with one gnarled hand and shoved his fingers through the few white strands clinging to the top of his head. "Strangest thing, Daniel. Two masked men park their van next to Ellie Brooks's car and wait for her to come out to the parking lot. They attack her and attempt to kidnap her foster child, Owen. Ellie fought them off long enough to lock herself in the SUV and call me. One attacker broke the window, but when I came running out of the church, they both took off in the van."

"Did you get a look at the license plate?"

"It didn't have one. White van, no lettering. The kind businesses use for deliveries." Irritation flashed. "I should've hopped in my cruiser and followed it, but my primary objective was making sure Miss Brooks and little Owen were all right."

"Rightfully so. How are they?"

"Shaken up, but uninjured, thanks be to God. Miss Brooks apparently is versed in martial arts. She broke one attacker's nose and popped the other in the knee. I've got alerts out to every hospital in a 100-mile radius in case our perpetrators seek medical treatment. So far, nothing."

Daniel's brow arched as he stepped toward the spray of dried blood on the light-colored asphalt next to an evidence marker. Appreciation sparked. "She got the guy good."

"Miss Brooks is only Owen's foster mom at the moment, but she loves him fiercely. She's already working through the process of adopting him." Pride layered Roy's voice, as if he was speaking about a treasured granddaughter.

Interesting. Who was the woman? She'd seemed to have captured the hearts of everyone in town. Daniel's mother was a softy, but Roy wasn't the mushy type, nor was he prone to giving undeserved compliments. "Witnesses?" Daniel asked.

"None. Owen was pretty upset and Miss Brooks was shaken, so I insisted both of them be examined by paramedics before being questioned."

Daniel's gaze swept over the glass littering the parking lot before shifting to the broken window. A sense of duty sank its claws into him. He'd been dragged into this case by his mother, but she'd been right to call him. Kidnapping a child took either guts or desperation. Sometimes both. The criminals needed to be caught. "Mind if I join you for the questioning?"

Roy grinned. "Not at all. In fact, take the lead."

"I don't want to step on your toes, sir—"

"Shut your trap. It'll be a pleasure to watch you in action." He winked. "Don't you worry. If you forget to ask something, I won't hesitate to jump in."

Daniel couldn't help the wry grin that crept across his lips. Roy would also never let him live it down.

They crossed the parking lot to the church annex. The squat, rectangular brick building was part Sunday school wing, part reception hall. It was functional, not pretty, with aging gutters and a faded mural of Noah's Ark on the side wall that had weathered more than a few Texas storms.

Inside, the main space had been transformed for the upcoming bazaar, booths arranged in a loose grid formation. Hand-lettered signs marked tables for baked goods, crafts, and silent auction items. Folding chairs lined the walls, and a plastic tote of half-unpacked decorations sat forgotten near the punch table.

It should've felt festive. Instead, the air was tight with tension.

A uniformed officer stood just inside the open door, hands resting on his duty belt, watching as EMTs packed up their gear and rolled it toward the exit. Roy gave his subordinate a nod before approaching the small children's nursery.

Daniel followed him inside, his gaze sweeping over the cribs along the west wall and the mural painted above cubbies filled with toys before landing on the woman seated on a built-in padded bench next to the window.

Ellie Brooks.

Training kicked in, prompting him to catalog her appearance. Slender, but athletic. Blonde hair, rich with shades both warm and cool, pulled into a ponytail that had mostly come undone. Her features were classically feminine—high forehead, delicate cheekbones, a graceful jawline—but there was nothing soft about the way she looked at him.

Their gazes met. Her eyes were a stormy gray, sharp and unreadable. Assessing him. Measuring.

Tough. That was the first word that came to Daniel's mind.

Not even the sleeping child nestled in her arms softened the impression. If anything, the way she held the boy with such calm steadiness only reinforced it. This woman had fought off two masked attackers with her bare hands. She hadn't curled up or fallen apart. She'd protected the kid, locked herself in the vehicle, and called it in.

Respect sparked first. Attraction came second, sharp and uninvited and immediate. He wasn't prepared for that.

Roy drew closer. "Miss Brooks—"

A sharp lift of Ellie's finger to her lips silenced the older man. "Keep your voice down, please, chief. Owen just fell asleep. If he wakes now, it'll be another hour of crying and none of us want that."

Roy gave a sharp nod and then whispered, "Allow me to introduce Texas Ranger Daniel Perez. He's assisting with the case and needs to ask you some questions."

"Perez." Ellie's head tilted, the strands of her ponytail drifting across one shoulder. "Marta's son?"

"Yes." Daniel pulled over a nearby chair and sat. "I've heard a lot about you, Miss Brooks. And Owen. I'm sorry we had to meet under these circumstances."

"Me too." She patted Owen's back lightly, but her assessing gaze never wavered. She was measuring him up. It was hard to tell if she found him lacking. "Your mom's told me a lot about you too. She's very proud of you."

"Being the firstborn means she's had decades to

polish my reputation. Though she tends to embellish quite a bit."

That earned him a light laugh, giving Daniel a moment to study the baby in her arms.

Owen's cheeks were blotchy from crying, his lashes still damp. A riot of blond curls framed his angelic face, soft and flushed with sleep. His small body was curled into Ellie's with complete, unguarded trust, one fist still gripping the ear of a tattered stuffed dog.

Something twisted low in Daniel's chest.

His gaze lifted to meet Ellie's. "Are you and Owen okay?"

"Physically, yes." Her voice was quiet and measured. "Owen's still young enough that I don't think he'll remember anything of what happened. I, on the other hand..."

She didn't finish the sentence. She didn't have to. The incident had shaken her. It was there in the way she held him. Fierce. Protective. As if she never intended to let go.

Daniel hated to make her relive it, but he didn't have a choice. "Can you tell me what happened?"

Ellie took him through the sequence of events with the practiced detachment Daniel had only seen in fellow law enforcement or military members. Every word was calm, even when she got to the harrowing part about the window shattering. Daniel took notes as she spoke, but his attention was on her word choice and her demeanor. "Can you describe the men who attacked you?"

"They were wearing ski masks, so I didn't see their

faces. Mr. Broken Nose was 5'8, around 210 pounds, Caucasian. He wore a black T-shirt and pants. No distinguishing tattoos or markings that I could see. The other guy was also Caucasian. Also wearing a black T-shirt and pants. Dozens of tattoos on his arms, more than I could catalog, but there was a distinctive dragon one on his right forearm." She pointed to the general area on her own arm. "It was red, the mouth pointed at his wrist. He was about 6'0 and 230 pounds."

Roy was busy scribbling all the information down, then he stepped back and pulled out his cell phone. Probably calling in the description to update the BOLO.

Daniel remained still, his pen hovering over the notebook in his lap. His eyes didn't leave Ellie. "You've described the perpetrators better than most cops I've worked with."

Her mouth flattened slightly and then she shrugged. "I'm a big fan of crime shows. And I'm a mystery writer. I notice things others miss."

"Right." Daniel wasn't quite buying that explanation, but he'd let it ride for now. "I forgot Mom told me you were a writer. She bought me one of your books for Christmas last year. I'm ashamed to admit I haven't read it yet. I don't get a lot of downtime."

Ellie didn't respond. The silence drew out, but she showed no external sign of discomfort. Finally, Daniel tapped his pen on his notepad. "You told Chief O'Neal the attackers were after Owen. How can you be sure of that?"

She didn't do it, but Daniel had the distinct impression she wanted to roll her eyes. "I told you, one attacker picked Owen up and tried to carry him away." Her jaw tightened. "If they wanted the car or money, they would've gone for my purse or demanded my keys. Neither did. They were after him. Trust me."

Daniel agreed with her logic. But he'd learned a long time ago never to jump to conclusions, especially in a case with this many unknowns.

Still, he'd follow the path she was leading him down. For now.

He flipped to a fresh page in his notebook. "Well, I guess that brings me to my next question. Can you think of any reason someone would want to kidnap Owen?"

THREE

She needed to be careful not to reveal too much.

Ellie traced circles on Owen's back, breathing in his baby powder scent. He was here. With her. Safe and content. But her mind couldn't stop playing out all the ways the attack could have gone differently, couldn't stop thinking about how close she came to losing this precious boy who'd captured her heart from the first moment she'd laid eyes on him.

Why God... why have You put me in this position?

It was a petulant question considering the good Lord above had spared her life along with Owen's. But Ellie was desperate for wisdom. She was walking a tightrope. The men who'd attacked her needed to be caught, but how much could she say without raising more questions? Daniel was already suspicious. Rightfully so. Ellie might've been able to convince everyone in town—including the police chief—that she'd worked for a publisher before

20

starting her career as a mystery writer, but it was all a lie. A fabrication designed to keep her and everyone around her safe.

In actuality, before moving to Silver Creek, she'd been a Special Agent with the FBI.

A phantom ache spread from the bullet wound in her side. The undercover operation had gone sideways without warning, leaving Ellie dying in a pool of her own blood. The doctors said it was a miracle she survived. But that miracle had come at a price. The criminal organization she'd been investigating had connections everywhere and a reputation for tying up loose ends. A hit was ordered before she went into surgery. By the time she came out of recovery, her death had already been reported to the media.

The Bureau hadn't corrected the story.

Only a handful of people knew she was alive—her direct supervisor, the witness protection coordinator, and the surgeon who'd saved her life. To the rest of the world, Special Agent Elizabeth Conway had died that night. The Bureau had moved quickly, giving her a new identity. A new life.

And so, Ellie Brooks, the mystery writer, was born.

Today's attack wasn't connected to her past. She was sure of it. She'd be dead if it was. No, Owen was the target and while Ellie had a theory about why, suggesting it might raise Daniel's suspicions even more. The handsome Texas Ranger had noticed how precisely she'd described the attackers. She'd slipped up there. A civilian would have struggled and been more vague. But in the aftermath of the attack, in order to keep herself calm, she'd relied on her training.

Old habits died hard.

"Miss Brooks." Daniel's voice cut into her thoughts. His pen was still poised over his pad, his gaze steady on her as if he was trying to decipher a puzzle she hadn't meant to offer. "You seemed lost in thought. Why don't you share what's running through your mind?"

"I was thinking about your question."

"Who would want to kidnap Owen?"

Ellie nodded. She continued to rub Owen's back gently, but purposefully let a little of the fear twisting her insides bleed into her voice. "I've read about baby trafficking rings while doing research for my books. They can be organized and are known to snatch kids in blitz-style attacks."

Daniel was quiet for a long moment. "Despite what you may see on television crime shows, stranger abductions are incredibly rare. I'm not ruling out the possibility, but it's more likely someone close to Owen is behind this. What do you know about his birth parents?"

"His mother died in childbirth and his father signed away his rights without ever meeting his son. Neither of them is responsible for this."

"And their families?"

Frustration built like a storm surge in her chest. A part of her knew these questions were relevant—Daniel was right that stranger abductions were rare—but it was annoying to follow a path she already knew led nowhere.

"I don't think either of Owen's parents had good home lives, and so far, no one in Owen's extended family has even requested to meet him. They don't care. Certainly not enough to hire two men to snatch him from a parking lot."

She sucked in a breath and calmed her voice. "Besides, if they wanted to raise him, all a family member would have to do is contact the caseworker. Family courts are partial to relatives. Unless the relative was unfit, Owen would be placed with his family."

Daniel uttered a noncommittal sound and arched a questioning brow. "How do you know the perpetrators who attacked you were hired criminals?"

Oh, Marta Perez hadn't raised a fool. Ellie forced herself to meet his gaze. "I don't know for certain. It was just... an impression."

The explanation sounded weak even to her own ears. Daniel's expression remained neutral, but something in his eyes suggested he wasn't convinced.

He didn't press, not right away.

Instead, he studied her for a beat longer, then shifted in his chair and jotted something in his notebook. The silence stretched out. Maybe he was attempting to rattle her? See what else she might say to fill the silence? It wouldn't work. Ellie had used the same tactic herself many times and was comfortable staying quiet.

She kept her hand on Owen's back as she studied the Texas Ranger across from her. She'd known he was a problem from the moment he walked in. Daniel had the kind of quiet authority that didn't need to announce itself. Everything about him suggested competence and control, from his steady dark eyes that missed very little to the questions he asked. His olive-toned skin was weathered just enough to suggest years in the sun, and his neatly trimmed dark hair carried a hint of silver at the temples.

He resembled Marta slightly, in the curve of his generous mouth and the way his brow furrowed when he concentrated, but unlike his mother's extroverted nature, Daniel was far more reserved. A product of his job, perhaps. It made him harder to read than most. Even now, Ellie couldn't quite tell what he was thinking.

Daniel glanced up and met her gaze. Suspicion darkened their color to a rich brown, but when he spoke, his tone was mild. "How long have you had Owen?"

"Since birth," she said. "He was placed with me directly from the hospital."

"Any unusual visitors at the house? Suspicious vehicles in the neighborhood? Calls or messages that felt... off?"

She shook her head. "Nothing."

"Has he been in the news recently? Featured in any public events?"

"No. I'm careful about things like that." She had to be. For her own sake.

Daniel leaned back slightly. His posture relaxed, but Ellie wasn't fooled. He was still watching her, still filing away every word. "Something made you think the perpetrators were hired. What gave you that impression?"

Ellie hesitated. They'd moved like professionals. One had gone for Owen, the other for her. It hadn't been messy or frenzied—not like something driven by emotion. It had been calculated and controlled. But she couldn't share all those observations, so she picked one that seemed reasonable for a mystery writer.

"It was their focus." Ellie purposefully creased her forehead, as if she was figuring out how to explain what she'd instinctively felt. "They didn't say a word. They didn't grab my purse, didn't ask for the keys. One reached straight for Owen, while the other came at me. It felt coordinated. Like they knew exactly what they were there for."

Daniel inclined his head thoughtfully. "And you think that kind of coordination points to a trafficking ring?"

"I think it's a possibility."

Again, he made that annoying noncommittal sound. Ellie felt that surge of frustration all over again. The first 24 hours of the investigation were critical. If Daniel spent his time focused on Owen's family or on her, he wouldn't find the culprits responsible for this attack.

Before she could say anything, Roy hung up his phone and hurried across the room. "We've got a lead on the van. A pharmacy in the next county was robbed by two men wearing ski masks. They took the cash from the register and some medical supplies. I'm heading over to the pharmacy to interview the witnesses." He turned to Daniel. "Want to join me?"

Daniel flipped his notebook closed. "I'll stay here and make sure Miss Brooks and Owen get home safely."

Oh no. He was going to use that opportunity to dig into her background. She was already on edge after the attack. The last thing she needed was a too-smart-for-his-own-good Texas Ranger digging for details about her past.

Maybe he was more like Marta than she'd given him credit for. Both were relentless when they noticed something wasn't right. Ellie had convinced the trusting Marta, along with everyone else in town, that she was exactly who she said, but she instinctively knew she'd met her match in Daniel Perez.

"There's no need to go out of your way, Ranger Perez." Ellie shifted to the edge of the window seat, trying hard not to jostle Owen too much. "We'll get home just fine on our own in my vehicle."

Daniel's hand landed on her elbow as she rose, a steadying counterbalance to the weight of the child in her arms. His touch was warm, his hold gentle and yet firm. Ellie's heart skipped a beat as her startled gaze lifted to his.

He smiled. "Daniel."

"Excuse me?" She was having trouble pulling together a thought while he was still touching her.

"You can call me Daniel." He released her elbow and stepped back. "Unfortunately, your SUV can't be moved until the crime scene is processed. I'm happy to take you and Owen myself."

"I can call someone." Her gaze shifted to Roy. "Or

I'm sure an officer or a sheriff's deputies will give me a lift."

"Everyone's busy." Roy clapped a hand on Daniel's shoulder. "This lawman is the only one not assigned to a task. Easier for everyone if he gives you a lift." The chief shot her a concerned look. "I know half a dozen people you can call to drive y'all home, but I'd feel a lot better knowing Daniel made sure you got there safe and sound. Save this old man from the extra worry, would ya, hon?"

Normally, Ellie would be irritated at being handled, but she sensed genuine worry in Roy's voice. She knew well enough when she'd been beaten. Besides, causing a fuss might make Roy wonder why she wasn't accepting help. Then she'd have two law enforcement officers digging into her past.

With a tight smile, Ellie nodded. "All right. Thank you, Ranger Perez. I'd appreciate a ride home."

As if he detected her brewing annoyance at being trapped into accepting his offer, Daniel's lips curved into a half-smile. He collected the diaper bag from the floor. "I know we just met, but my mother calls herself Owen's godmother. There's no need for formality. Please call me Daniel."

He was trying to lower her guard. She knew the game well and was tempted to ignore his request, but that would be more than rude. Instead, she gave him a saccharine smile. "You can call me Ellie."

Those handsome lips twitched with amusement, and then he gestured toward the door. "After you, Ellie."

His voice was deep and carried a rhythm she couldn't

quite place. Not distinctly Texan, not fully Latino either. Smooth and low. A little smoky. Ellie liked it, and that irritated her beyond measure.

"Wait." Roy crossed the nursery class, opened a closet door, and removed a car seat. "You'll need this. I'll let Mrs. Jenkins know you'll be borrowing it for a few days."

Warmth spread through Ellie. This is why she loved Silver Creek. No one hesitated a moment to help a fellow neighbor. "Thank you for thinking of it, Roy." She fell into step beside him as they left the nursery. "How long before I can get my SUV?"

"You'll have it tomorrow morning. I'll have your window replaced, and then one of my officers will drive it over to your house."

Roy held open the main door for her, giving Ellie a momentary flashback of the moments before the attack. Her breath hitched, and she hugged Owen tighter against her. Automatically, her gaze scanned the parking lot. A few law enforcement officers lingered, but most of the crowd behind the yellow crime scene tape had dispersed. Still, a shiver raced down her spine.

She felt exposed. Were there eyes on her? Or was it her imagination?

Ellie hadn't touched a gun since being shot, but right now, she wished for her trusty Glock.

As if he sensed her fear, Daniel stepped alongside her so that she was flanked between him and Roy as they crossed the lot to a Ford Explorer marked with official law enforcement decals. With surprisingly quick efficiency, Daniel secured the car seat. Perhaps he'd had a lot of practice. He had scads of nieces and nephews.

Roy lightly touched Ellie's shoulder before she got into the vehicle. "If you have any trouble tonight, call the station. I'll have my night-duty officers make extra loops in your neighborhood, so don't be concerned if you spot them coming and going."

His words were meant to be reassuring, but they only heightened Ellie's concern. Why had Owen been targeted? She felt strongly they were hired guns—maybe part of a criminal enterprise—but her gut instinct wasn't proof. There was no guarantee the danger was over. Not until the perpetrators were caught. And maybe not even then.

She worried at her bottom lip. "Please let me know if you make an arrest."

"You'll be one of my first calls."

She'd have to be satisfied with that. Ellie carefully laid Owen down in the car seat and strapped him in. The little boy didn't so much as sigh. He was completely out. She settled in the seat next to him and tucked back one of his runaway curls, her chest tightening with emotion. Even in his sleep, Owen held fast to his trusted stuffed dog, Scout.

The tender moment was broken as Daniel slid into the driver's seat and turned back to face her. "All strapped in?"

"Yep. Ready to go."

As he fired up the engine, she mentally braced herself for the questions that would come. Somehow, during this car ride, she had to convince Daniel that he needed to focus his attention on the men who tried to kidnap Owen, and not on her.

Her baby's life could depend on it.

FOUR

Daniel glanced in the rearview mirror. Ellie was staring out the window into the night, her expression pensive as they turned out of the church parking lot. But there was something fragile beneath that controlled exterior, a contradiction to the rigid line of her shoulders.

The woman had secrets. That much Daniel was certain of. But did they pertain to the attack on her and Owen? He wasn't sure. Considering their interaction at the church, it would be difficult to get Ellie to open up, but he had to try. The more he learned about the attack at the church, the more concerned he became about Owen's safety.

Daniel eased to a stop for a red light. He pointed toward the feed store at the corner. "My first job was at Jake's. I was thirteen, hired to sweep floors and stock shelves on the weekend. It turned out to be a complete catastrophe."

He caught Ellie's gaze in the rearview mirror. She arched a brow in silent invitation for him to continue.

"One morning, I forgot to lock the back gate. Twenty-seven goats got loose, devouring several flowerbeds and nearly causing a three-car pileup before trotting straight down Main Street to interrupt the mayor's reelection speech."

Her mouth dropped open. "That was you! I've heard about the incident, but everyone described the kid responsible as just 'the youngster'."

He chuckled. "It was me all right. A photographer caught me mid-chase during the mayor's speech. The newspaper put it on the front page. My mom still has the clipping somewhere." The light turned green, and Daniel accelerated. "Needless to say, I wasn't allowed anywhere near the livestock after that."

He heard her faint chuckle and was pleased to see, when he glanced in the back seat, that the tension in her shoulders had eased. Daniel focused back on the road as he followed the GPS to Ellie's subdivision. "How long have you lived in Silver Creek?"

"Three years."

"Ah. Long enough to hear most of the folklore, including the great goat escapade." Daniel combed through his brain, trying to remember the details his mom had shared about Ellie during their phone calls. He suspected Marta was playing matchmaker at the time, and had tuned out most of it, but some things stuck. "Before that, you lived in Austin, right? Is that where your folks are?"

"No. My parents passed shortly after I graduated college."

Her tone was taut with a pain he recognized. Daniel briefly met her gaze in the rearview mirror. "I'm sorry to hear that. We lost my dad five years ago. It's the kind of loss that stays with you."

She nodded but didn't reply. Daniel reduced his speed for another red light just as Ellie laid her head back against the headrest and closed her eyes. Her polite, nonverbal way of telling him to shut up. Daniel was secretly amused by the tactic. Ellie knew he was doing his best to put her at ease and then dig into her past. Her ability to anticipate his maneuvers... her description of the perpetrators... the way she'd fought back during the attack...

If he didn't know any better, he'd peg her for a cop.

A whimper rose from the back seat. Ellie's eyes instantly snapped open, and she bent over Owen's car seat. "Shhh, sweet boy. It's okay."

The cry fell silent. Daniel pressed on the gas as the light changed. "Is Owen okay?"

"He cries out sometimes in his sleep. I always worry he's having nightmares." She sighed. "He's been through a lot."

Daniel hesitated and then said gently, "Mom mentioned he has a heart condition. She asked me to pray for Owen when he had surgery a few months back."

Ellie gave a slight nod, her gaze dropping to the sleeping boy in the car seat. "He was born with Tetralogy of Fallot. It's a congenital defect—four structural problems with the heart, all at once. It affects the way blood flows through the body, making it hard for him to get enough oxygen."

Daniel's hands tightened on the steering wheel. "That sounds serious."

"It is. Thankfully, Owen was strong enough to undergo a complete repair at seven months. He'll never play professional sports, and he may need another surgery later in life, but for the most part, he's perfectly fine now. A bit delayed in his development, but that's normal for TOF babies." She smiled down at Owen. "He started crawling only last month, but he's already standing up on his own and doing his best to walk."

The love in her voice reached deep into Daniel's heart, squeezing it tight. Ellie might be keeping secrets, but her devotion to Owen was obvious. "He's lucky to have you in his corner. What made you decide to become a foster mom?"

Ellie seemed to consider her next words carefully. "Being a foster mom is an opportunity to be a part of something bigger than myself. Providing safety, love, and care to a child who—through no fault of their own—was put into a bad situation can change everything for them." She glanced at Owen again. "What I didn't expect was how much it would make a difference in my life."

"The sleepless nights? The smelly diapers?"

She laughed. "Yes, that too. But Owen's made me softer somehow, and he's shown me there's no limit in my capacity to love." Ellie paused. "That sounds cheesy, doesn't it?"

He chuckled. "It sounds like a mom." Daniel waited a beat. This avenue of conversation wasn't revealing much about Ellie's past, but it was giving him a sense of who she was. And the more he saw, the more he liked. No wonder the entire town adored her. "It couldn't have been easy, taking on a sick baby by yourself. You weren't scared?"

"I was terrified. Most people have nine months to prepare. I had two hours' warning that Owen was coming home with me. But once word got out that I had a newborn, my doorbell started ringing. Marta brought over clothes and babysat so I could catch a catnap. Virginia organized a few ladies at church to pop in and clean my house, and the sewing circle made enough casseroles to fill my freezer two times over. Everyone in Silver Creek adores Owen, and I'm grateful we have so many good people around us."

She grew quiet and pensive, her gaze drifting to the window and the trees lining the side of the country road. A stiffness in her jaw indicated she was thinking the same thing Daniel was. His voice was sympathetic as he said, "It makes the attack today even more shocking."

"Yes." She tilted her head to one side. "How long have you been with the Texas Rangers?"

"Twelve years. I worked for the Criminal Investigations Division before that, specializing in organized crime."

Daniel let that settle between them as he turned into a neighborhood filled with cookie-cutter style homes. It was one of the newer developments in Silver Creek.

There was a sprawling park, a swimming pool, a cabana for hosting events, and bike paths. Mature trees lined the sidewalk, providing shade in the summer.

Ellie's house was at the end of a cul-de-sac. It was one story with a tiny front porch and neatly trimmed grass. Her porch light was on, illuminating a hanging plant next to her front door. Daniel pulled into the driveway and killed the engine. He twisted in his seat to face her.

"Based on my experience investigating organized crime, snatching children off the streets is rare. Human trafficking rings prefer easy marks. Homeless teens they can turn into baby-making machines, for example. They prey on those who can't defend themselves, and as a general rule, don't want to call too much attention to themselves. Kidnapping a medically challenged child in broad daylight in the middle of a church parking lot... it doesn't fit the mold." He met her gaze in the semi-darkness. Held it. "This feels personal. So I need to know, are you involved in something criminal? Is there any reason someone would want to hurt you by kidnapping Owen?"

Ellie's eyes narrowed, just slightly. "No." Her voice was steady, but a flicker of hurt crossed her face. "There's nothing in this world I love more than Owen. If I thought for one moment this had something to do with me, I would tell you."

Sincerity coated every word. Daniel believed her but couldn't shake the feeling there was more to the kidnapping. "Could be an ex-boyfriend, maybe."

She snorted in reply. "I haven't dated in years. Trust me, none of my exes are paying attention to anything I'm doing." Ellie's hand went to the door handle, but then she paused and her voice grew quiet. "I know it's farfetched, but I believe those men were hired to kidnap Owen. Why? I can't say. The only thing that makes any sense is that someone wants him. It could be a woman who can't have a child. Or a baby-selling ring. Most crimes follow patterns, but there are exceptions."

"And you know this because of all the research you do for your mystery books." His tone was dry, and Daniel didn't even attempt to hide his sarcasm.

Ellie didn't even blink. "Yep."

The woman could lie. He'd give her that. There wasn't even a flicker of hesitation in her expression. It certainly made his job a lot harder. Daniel believed she had Owen's best interests at heart, but he wasn't entirely sure she was seeing the case clearly.

Before he could formulate another question, Ellie opened the door and hopped out of the vehicle. Within seconds, she had the car seat free too.

He grabbed the diaper bag and joined her on the walkway. The night air was crisp, the temperature dropping quickly now that evening was settling in. A car engine roared on a nearby street, sending a jolt of awareness through Daniel's nerves. Something was wrong. He placed a hand on Ellie's arm, stopping her before she reached the porch.

"Wait." Daniel scanned the property, trying to figure out what had triggered his instincts.

That's when he noticed the shattered windowpane just beyond the glow of the porch light. The diaper bag hit the ground with a thump as he pulled his weapon from its holster.

Someone had broken into Ellie's house.

And they might still be inside.

Lying in wait.

FIVE

Ellie stared at the broken window as fear coursed through her body.

This couldn't be happening. It just... couldn't be.

"Ellie." Daniel's tone was sharp but hushed. His hand still on her arm, he guided her several steps away from the front door until they were around the corner of the house, out of sight of anyone inside. "Take Owen back to my Explorer and lock the doors. Call 911 to report the break-in. Make sure you tell dispatch I'm on scene. Where are your house keys?"

"In the front pocket of the diaper bag." Her gaze darted to his. Years of professional training overrode her fear as she snapped into cop mode. "You shouldn't go in without backup."

"Thanks for the advice, but if there's a way to stop this now, I'm taking it."

The weight of Owen in his carrier was heavy, her primary responsibility clear. Yet her heart lurched at the thought of Daniel entering the house and confronting an intruder. "Daniel—"

"Car. Locks. 911." His tone brooked no argument. Daniel's head tilted toward his Explorer in the driveway. "Now, Ellie."

Stubborn, infuriating man. She knew better than most how quickly an operation could go wrong. But what was she going to do? Wrestle him to the ground and hold him there until backup arrived? She had Owen to think about, and he had to be her priority. "Don't get yourself killed, or Marta will never forgive me."

His deep chuckle followed her down the driveway. She eased open the passenger-side rear door and set Owen—car seat and all—inside on the floor before climbing into the vehicle and shutting the door. The locks snicked into place with a flip of a button. Daniel waited one minute more, probably to ensure she wouldn't come back out, and then eased toward the house. The porch light glinted off the gun in his hand.

Her breath stalled. Ellie fumbled for her cell phone, pulling it from her pocket. She dialed 911 and rattled off information to the dispatcher while watching Daniel.

He moved with practiced precision toward the diaper bag before slipping onto the porch. Every move was measured and purposeful. Early in her career, Ellie had a trainer who said you could tell a lot about a law enforcement officer by how they handled stress. Some rushed in without thinking. Others hesitated too long, caught in the what-ifs. But the best—the ones you trusted to have your back—struck a balance. They made fast, decisive calls based on the facts at hand and then moved forward, always willing to adjust the plan as needed.

From the way Daniel approached the house, Ellie knew he fell into the third group. He was comfortable taking risks, but he wasn't reckless about it. Still, it didn't stop her pulse from racing as he entered the dark recesses of the house.

After all, she'd been in that third group too. And she'd ended up shot.

"Officers are en route, ma'am." The dispatcher's voice cut through Ellie's thoughts. "Please keep this line open until they arrive."

Owen took that moment to send up a wail of distress. Ellie put the call on speaker and then undid the straps holding him in the car seat before lifting him into her arms. His back was warm and slightly sweaty, the onesie sticking to his skin. Poor boy was probably hungry. She'd given him a bottle at the church after the attack, but he'd missed dinner entirely.

"Shhh, shhhh, sweet boy. It's going to be okay." Ellie rocked gently in the seat, even as her attention shifted between the familiar neighborhood street and her front door. Where was Daniel? She hadn't heard gunshots, which was a relief, but that didn't mean he was safe.

Please, Lord. Protect Daniel.

For the second time today, she was locked in a vehicle with a crying child, praying. Frustration, piping hot, sliced through her. This part of her life was supposed to be over. The danger and fear. The constant worry. She'd left all of it behind with her FBI career. It hadn't been easy to settle into life in Silver Creek. Trusting people again had taken time. Now that hard-won security was being ripped away. Worse—her child was in harm's way.

And for what?

Why was this happening?

Ellie couldn't make heads or tails of it.

Had the Iron Fist found her? It wasn't impossible, but considering the measures she took to keep herself safe, it seemed unlikely. Besides, they wanted her dead. There would be no reason to kidnap Owen or break into her house. At least, none that she could think of. Still, that thought didn't erase the pit of fear that'd settled in her stomach or the nagging feeling that she was engaging in wishful thinking.

Stop. She couldn't allow illogical fear to send her into a tailspin of hypotheticals. She needed to analyze the facts. Needed to *think*. But that wouldn't happen with a baby crying in her ear and Daniel still in the house.

Owen's food was in the diaper bag sitting on the driveway. She didn't dare risk getting out of the vehicle to retrieve it. Instead, Ellie alternated between gentle bounces and slow side-to-side movements, continuing to whisper soothing words even as she watched the front door. Owen's cries lessened to heartbreaking whimpers. She brushed away the tears on his cheeks with her thumb. "There. There. Everything is going to be okay."

Simple words. A promise Ellie wasn't sure she could keep.

Daniel exited the house, his weapon holstered. A burst of relief flooded through Ellie, but it was short-lived as she took in his furrowed brow. She exited the Explorer into the cool night air, carrying Owen in her arms, and intercepted Daniel on the driveway. "Backup is on the way. What happened? Did someone break in?"

"They sure did. And they weren't subtle."

"What does that mean?" Rather than wait for his reply, Ellie sidestepped him. She hurried up the walkway. Her front door was open, the light in the kitchen illuminating the open-concept floor plan.

She gasped.

Her house had been ransacked.

Glass from picture frames she'd hung on the wall littered the wood floor. The cushions on her couch had been sliced open, the stuffing flung around the living room like a tornado of clouds. Books were ripped open, dishes smashed. Every drawer had been gone through. Her television had been ripped from the wall and broken into pieces. Nothing was left untouched. Even pieces of the floor had been pried up to reveal the subfloor underneath.

Owen on her hip, Ellie stood in the center of her destroyed house and turned in a circle, taking in the destruction. Indignation burned in her chest. They were only things, but they were *her* things. She'd refinished the bookcase by hand, chosen throw blankets to match her dishes, and nursed an ivy plant until it covered her cabinets.

All of it gone in the blink of an eye.

"Don't touch anything." Glass crunched under

Daniel's cowboy boots as he entered the house behind her. "It's a crime scene."

"I'm aware," Ellie snapped. She didn't have the patience or the emotional control to measure her tone. Fury was the only thing keeping her from bursting into tears. "Is the entire house like this?"

Sympathy flashed across his handsome features. "Yes. It doesn't appear the intruders took anything, although you'll have to go through the house to be sure."

Anger vibrated through her. The only thing worse than seeing her living room in total chaos was knowing that Owen's beautiful nursery was also destroyed. It normally took a lot to get a rise out of Ellie, but today had broken through the tight walls of control she kept on her emotions.

The baby whimpered, likely picking up on Ellie's tension. She forced herself to take a deep breath and wrangle herself back under control. She pressed her lips to Owen's cheek and cupped the back of his head. Ellie could be mad later. Right now, she needed to think like a cop. "Did the men who attacked me in the parking lot do this?"

"Too early to say. If they did, it was before the attack. I doubt either of them was interested in breaking into your house with an aching knee and a broken nose." Daniel leveled a look in her direction. "Whoever it was, they didn't steal any electronics. This wasn't done by someone looking to make a quick buck."

Ellie agreed with his assessment. Sirens wailed in the distance.

"I don't understand. Why would someone break into my house, search it, and then try to kidnap my foster child..."

The pieces snapped together as she said it aloud.

Her stomach tightened with dread. "They were searching for something." Her voice dropped to a whisper as the realization detonated like a bomb. "Something they didn't find."

"Yes." His tone was grave as he gestured toward the fireplace. "They left a message."

She turned and her blood ran cold.

A teddy bear had been taken from Owen's room. The animal's head had been nearly severed and hung loosely to one side. Stuffing poked out, stark against the mantel's dark wood. A note had been attached to the bear's chest by a knife from her kitchen. On unsteady legs, she stepped closer to read the hastily scrawled message.

We know you have it. Give it to us.

Or else.

The threat was clear. The men who'd attacked her today had meant for Ellie to find this message *after* Owen was kidnapped. Whatever they were looking for, however, she couldn't give them. She didn't know what it was.

She blinked and realized Daniel was standing directly in front of her. His gaze was intense, his attention fixed on her as his hands came to rest on her biceps. Owen was nestled between them.

"I know you don't want to believe this, but you're the

target, Ellie. *You.* So I need to know what you're hiding. It's the only way I can protect you and Owen."

SIX

Ellie watched as the sun rose over the Perez family ranch. Golden rays spilled across the hilltops like melted gold, painting the fence posts and the barn with an ethereal glow. Wildflowers carpeted the fields. A few delicate clouds drifted across the sky, and at this early hour, the moon was still faintly visible. Ranch hands escorted horses into the fields to graze. In the distance, greenhouses dotted the landscape.

Peaceful. It was the only word to describe it. But this morning, Ellie felt none of the serenity she'd prayed for.

She glanced at Owen, nestled in the portable crib set up in the corner of the guest room. He was on his side, one arm slung across his trusted dog, Scout. Long lashes kissed chubby cheeks. His breathing remained deep and even, his sleep undisturbed by yesterday's terrifying events.

Ellie gripped the cell in her hand and willed it to ring. She'd retrieved the burner phone from its hiding place, a secret pocket in the diaper bag, and dialed the only phone number programmed into it. An emergency line given to her by her former boss when the FBI erased her old identity. She'd left a message on the voice mail hours ago. No one had replied.

Maybe she was overreacting. Ellie wasn't one for wishful thinking, but she kept hoping the break-in and attempted kidnapping were unrelated to her failed undercover mission. Deep down, she knew that wasn't the case. The Iron Fist had found her, and the only reason she was still breathing was because she had something they wanted. Or, at least, they believed so.

What were they looking for? How had they even found her? Ellie couldn't answer either question, and at the moment, it didn't matter. Her priority was keeping Owen safe. It was why she'd accepted Daniel's offer to stay on his family ranch last night. The location was surrounded by fields, making it difficult to approach unseen, and was outfitted with a top-notch security system. It'd bought her a little time.

But the clock was ticking. With every second that passed, Ellie was put in a more precarious position.

She couldn't dodge Daniel's questions for much longer. But telling him the truth could expose him to danger, making him a target of the criminal organization. She had no idea what they were searching for or who was involved. The leader, Gideon Voss, had money and influence. It'd long been suspected he had moles buried in law enforcement and federal agencies.

Ellie didn't doubt Daniel's integrity for a moment.

He was Marta's son, for one. And last night, he'd proven that his only concern was keeping her and Owen safe. But his superiors? She didn't trust them at all. Once Daniel reported what he knew, the information would move up the chain of command. And God only knew how far it would go or who might hear it.

No. There was a protocol for this type of situation, and she had to follow orders.

Ellie dialed the emergency number again. With each ring, she willed someone to pick up.

No one did.

She nearly cursed aloud but caught herself. Instead, Ellie left another message, her voice low but sharp with urgency. "This is Special Agent Elizabeth Conway. I've been compromised and need immediate extraction for me and my foster son, Owen. We're both in danger. Repeat—my identity has been compromised. I've been attacked and my home broken into. I need instructions on the next steps and can't wait much longer."

She ended the call and swallowed down the fear and frustration rising in her throat. Closing her eyes, she drew in a deep breath.

"God, I could really use your guidance here. I don't know what to do or where to turn. Please help me keep my little boy safe."

Owen was all that mattered.

She had to protect him, no matter the cost.

When Ellie opened her eyes, Owen was standing at the edge of his crib. His gaze was still sleepy, but he offered her a crooked smile that tugged at her heartstrings. She tucked the burner phone into her pocket and crossed the room.

"Good morning, sweetie. Did you sleep well?"

Owen babbled in reply. He hadn't started talking yet, but he was a vocal baby. Ellie suspected once he found his words, he'd never stop. They kept up a steady stream of "conversation" as she changed his diaper and dressed him for the day. Playing peek-a-boo earned a peal of giggles that cut through every worry clawing at her mind.

For a little while, she let herself pretend everything was normal.

The smell of coffee and bacon drew her toward the kitchen with Owen in her arms. Marta stood at the counter, spooning creamy yogurt into a parfait glass layered with preserves. Her cheeks crinkled as she smiled. "Good morning, you two. You're just in time for breakfast."

Ellie's eyes widened at the spread on the table—pancakes, eggs, bacon, fresh biscuits, and fruit salad. "You made enough for an army." She sat Owen in the high chair and strapped him in. He immediately reached for Scout. She handed the stuffed dog over. "Are we expecting company?"

Marta laughed. "I overdo it when there are guests. Eat as much as you like. I'll send the rest down to the ranch hands. They'll be thrilled." She wiped her hands on a lemon-printed apron and handed Ellie a mug of coffee. "Creamer and sugar are on the table."

"Black is fine, thanks."

"That's right. You drink it like Daniel does."

"Who's talking about me again?" Daniel's voice came from the mud room.

A second later, he filled the doorway. He was dressed for ranch work in worn jeans and a checkered shirt that had seen better days. Hat hair and morning stubble gave him a rumpled look that was oddly reassuring, though the weapon at his hip reminded her to stay cautious. He was a Texas Ranger, and she couldn't reveal too much.

"Don't worry, son. I wasn't sharing any stories of your juvenile antics." Marta poured another cup of coffee and handed it to him. "I was simply telling Ellie that you and her both drink your coffee black."

"Is that so?"

Ellie's pulse quickened as their eyes connected. Daniel's smile didn't lose a smidge of its friendliness, but there was a wariness buried in his dark brown eyes. Nerves jittered her insides. She shouldn't care what he thought of her. They'd just met yesterday. And yet... she didn't like the fact that he didn't trust her.

Marta's dog, Jinx, squeezed past Daniel and bounded into the kitchen. The golden lab made a beeline for Owen, his black nose nudging the little boy's chubby legs. Owen giggled and leaned forward in the high chair to get a better look at the dog. Jinx's tail wagged like a metronome.

"Someone is hoping for scraps." Daniel settled into a chair at the table next to Owen. He tousled the baby's mop of curls. "What do you think, little man? Plan on sharing your breakfast with the dog?"

Owen bounced in his high chair and spoke gibberish

in reply. Despite the tension running through her, Ellie couldn't help but smile. "Jinx and Owen are good friends. They always share."

She reached for a fluffy, golden pancake and broke it into bite-sized pieces, setting them on the high chair tray. Owen promptly shoved one piece in his mouth and chewed on it, then tossed another to Jinx. The dog caught it midair.

Ellie laughed. "See?"

Daniel chuckled, but none of the wariness in his gaze disappeared. Ellie could feel his unspoken questions and mistrust, like an itch between her shoulder blades. There was a storm brewing, and she didn't know if it could be avoided.

Marta brought over the finished parfaits. The food was blessed, and everyone dug in. Thankfully, the older woman's bubbly personality kept the conversation flowing. By the time everyone finished eating, Owen was covered in eggs, bits of pancake, and yogurt. The dinosaur bib around his neck had saved his shirt from being stained with food, but his pants were a lost cause.

Ellie unstrapped him from the high chair. "Why on earth did I dress you? I should've waited until after breakfast was over."

Marta clapped her palms together and then reached for Owen. "Give that baby to me. I'll clean him up."

Oh no. Ellie didn't want to be left alone in the kitchen with Daniel. She pulled Owen closer. "I've got it—"

"Nonsense. You hardly ever get a break." Marta

swooped in and snatched Owen with the stealth of an operative. "Sit down. Have another cup of coffee." She smothered Owen's cheeks with kisses, and he giggled with joy. "We'll be back in two shakes of a lamb's tail. Won't we? Won't we?"

Ellie smiled and shook her head. She'd be lucky to touch Owen again today. Marta would keep him all to herself given half a chance.

Sadness followed the thought. Once the FBI got her message, they would extract her and Owen. They'd leave Silver Creek, and everyone in the town, behind. No one would know where they went or even if they were okay. Marta would be heartbroken.

The kitchen door swung shut, and the silence that followed was deafening.

Daniel sipped his coffee as if he didn't have a care in the world, but she could feel him watching her. Stupidly, her cheeks heated. Ellie began clearing the table, letting her hair fall over her face to hide her blush. "Has there been any word from Chief O'Neal? I was hoping the men who attacked me would be arrested by now."

"Unfortunately not. After robbing the pharmacy, the perpetrators took off in their van and haven't been seen since. The chief interviewed everyone at the pharmacy, but no one got a good look at either man since they were wearing masks. We've extended the BOLO to the entire state and alerted every hospital in Texas, but so far, nothing."

She dumped the dirty plates in the sink and flipped on the water. "You'd think Mr. Broken Nose would need medical treatment. I suppose he could have driven out of state to get it."

Daniel hummed in agreement. He joined her at the sink, flipping off the water and invading her personal space. She retreated instinctively and found herself cornered between the cabinet and the fridge. Daniel turned to face her, his stare sharp and probing. "Where were you born, Ellie?"

His question sent a wave of panic racing through her, but she jutted up her chin in defiance. "What does that matter?"

"Answer the question."

She folded her arms defensively. "I don't appreciate being interrogated."

"And I don't appreciate being lied to," he snapped. "According to a background check, you were born and raised in Liberty County, but according to the local hospital records, Ellie Brooks doesn't exist."

Her muscles tensed as anger filled her voice. "You dug into my past."

"What other choice did you leave me?" There was no regret in his expression, just hard determination. Daniel boxed her in, his broad shoulders blocking out everything but him. "Your real name isn't Ellie Brooks, is it? Your background check clears, but scratch the surface and there are holes bigger than the Grand Canyon. So I'll ask you again, what are you hiding?"

The sharp bite of panic cut through her anger. "Stop. You don't know what you're doing."

"I know exactly what I'm doing." His finger jabbed

toward the open doorway, anger flaring in his eyes. "I'm protecting that little boy in there. I have half a mind to call Child Protective Services and report you for fraud—"

"No!" Ellie's breathing became shallow. She couldn't lose Owen. Desperation flooded over her, threatening to drown her in its wake. She pinched the bridge of her nose to keep the tears at bay. Still, they thickened her voice. "Please, Daniel."

She drew a shaky breath, trying to rein in her spiraling emotions. This was so unlike her... to become overwhelmed by her feelings. But the stress of the last twenty-four hours, along with a sleepless night and Daniel's threats, were unraveling the last of her control.

The burner phone weighed heavily in her pocket. Ellie didn't know what to do. She was trapped between a rock and a hard place. Quite literally, by the unyielding countertop behind her and Daniel's broad body in front of her. Telling him the truth wasn't possible, but she couldn't refuse to answer all of his questions either.

She lifted her gaze to meet his and licked her lips. "I know it's hard for you to understand, but there are things I can't tell you. Things I can't explain. You have a job to do, I know that. But I need you to stop digging into my past and asking questions."

His eyes tracked over her face. "Are you a criminal? A former informant?"

"Neither. I swear it."

He scowled. "Forgive me, *Ellie Brooks*, but your *word* doesn't mean much."

She swallowed hard. "I know. But I swear on Owen's

life, I'm neither a criminal nor a former informant. I'm in a bad situation, and you know from the fact that my background check cleared, that my identity isn't stolen." Ellie gave him a pointed look. "I had help."

A beat passed. He cocked his head to one side. "You're not in witness protection. Otherwise, Federal Marshals would be beating down my door right now."

He was right about that. Ellie wished the FBI had gone that route, but they didn't want to use another federal agency in case the Iron Fist had informants among their ranks. The fewer people that knew about her new identity, the less likely it would be found out.

So much for that plan.

"There's only a few agencies capable of creating a brand-new identity while burying any trace of it in red tape...." One eyebrow arched. "You're FBI. Or CIA. Former military."

He was in the ballpark. That would have to be close enough. She gripped the counter behind her. "I can't answer that."

He nodded slowly, as if a puzzle piece had fallen into place anyway. "Do you know what those men were looking for?"

"No."

"But you know who they are?"

Ellie grimaced. "Mr. Broken Nose and Busted Kneecap, no, I don't know who they are."

"But you know who hired them?"

"I can't say."

"Unacceptable." Daniel's gaze narrowed. "How am I

supposed to protect you and Owen with a blindfold on and my hands tied behind my back? You need to give me something to work with, Ellie."

"I wish I could." Her jaw tightened to keep the truth from spilling past her lips. In this moment, she wanted to share everything. To lay her burdens down, let this handsome and capable Texas Ranger help her find a way out of this mess. It was a shock to realize how much she wanted that. Ellie wasn't used to relying on people. Silver Creek had softened her. Maybe too much. "I need you to give me a little leeway here."

"A little leeway?" He stared at her in disbelief. "You're asking me to blindly trust you without offering the same trust in return."

It was a lot. She knew better than most how much. "Not blindly. You know enough to make reasonable assumptions about the situation. Honestly, I've said more than I should." Ellie met his gaze. "I'm doing my best to keep everyone safe. You. Me. Most importantly, Owen."

"And how does this end? You can't hide out here at the ranch forever, and if what I suspect is true, whoever came after you and Owen won't stop."

"I've set things in motion. Hopefully, I'll have answers soon."

He huffed out a frustrated breath. "That's cryptic." Daniel studied her for a long moment, his mouth flattened, his expression uncertain. And then, whatever decision he was wrestling with seemed to be made because his shoulders dropped and he backed up a step. "You have till the end of the day. Tomorrow, I'll need more."

She breathed out. "That's fair. Thank you, Daniel. I—"

Her next words were cut off by an alert from her smart watch. She glanced at the screen and groaned. "Owen has a doctor's appointment today."

"Cancel it." Daniel's brow furrowed. "Leaving the ranch is too dangerous."

Her mind whirled. "If it was a check-up with his pediatrician, I would, but this is an appointment with his cardiac specialist. He needs to go." Especially if she and Owen were removed from Silver Creek. It could be months before he could get a new appointment with another cardiologist. "It should be quick. An hour at most. His doctor is nearby, at Mercy Hospital. I strongly doubt anyone from—"

She cut herself off from saying 'the Iron Fist' at the last minute. Ellie considered her options. "The chances of Mr. Broken Nose and his companion figuring out we have a doctor's appointment is slim to none. We'll be safe."

"What about whoever hired those men?"

"Same." She prayed that was true. It had to be. "I wouldn't go unless it was important. Owen's condition requires regular check-ins with his specialist in case a complication arises. We can't skip it."

Daniel exhaled slowly, his jaw tight. "Then I'm coming with you."

SEVEN

Mercy Hospital was located halfway between Houston and Silver Creek. The bustling complex consisted of an emergency room, outpatient care, and doctors' offices. Daniel had done a quick sweep of the area after they checked in, but the tension in his shoulders hadn't eased.

He kept a steady eye on Ellie and Owen in the small play area across the waiting room. They were stacking wooden blocks. Owen was intensely focused on balancing one more piece on the growing tower. His brow furrowed with toddler determination, one hand holding fast to his tattered stuffed dog. Then, with a decisive swipe, he knocked the tower over and giggled.

Ellie laughed too, her head tilted back slightly, the soft sound chasing away some of the weight in Daniel's chest. It was a sweet moment. Pure and unguarded. If he hadn't been so on edge, Daniel might've smiled. Instead, he kept his voice pitched low as he pressed his cell phone to his ear.

"I don't know her real identity. Not yet. I'm working on that."

Texas Ranger Cole Donnelly exhaled a long breath on the other end. "So you're asking me to come to your ranch to help guard a woman whose real name you don't know? And a baby who's technically in state custody." A pause. "You do realize your first call should've been to Child Protective Services?"

Daniel's jaw tightened. "I'm aware, Cole. I didn't call for a lecture."

"No, you called for help. And if I'm putting myself on the line, I'd like to know what I'm stepping into."

"You're right. I'm sorry." Daniel drew in a breath and let it out slowly. Despite Daniel being the oldest member of Company A and Cole the youngest, they'd formed a friendship built on mutual respect. "Normally, I would've called CPS, but nothing about this case fits, and until I know more, I want to keep Owen close. Whoever's after Ellie tried to use that baby as leverage. They're looking for something."

"But you don't know what?"

"No."

He looked back toward the play area. Ellie was helping Owen to build a new tower of blocks. Her sunshine locks were tucked into a braid that spilled over one shoulder. No makeup. Somehow, she made the practical jeans and T-shirt look both effortless and elegant. Owen knocked over the block tower, and Ellie laughed before tickling him. The smile on her face nearly stole Daniel's breath.

He stamped down the attraction immediately. No way. No how.

The woman was easily fifteen years younger, living a lie, and completely wrong for him. He had a job to do, and getting distracted by wayward feelings wouldn't help anyone.

As if she felt his gaze, Ellie looked up. Her striking gray eyes clouded instantly with worry. Daniel offered a reassuring smile and turned his attention back to the call.

"She's scared, Cole. Terrified, actually. If I had to hazard a guess, I think she's former law enforcement. Maybe FBI. Whoever is after her and Owen sent his cronies to do the job. If it's a gang or criminal organization, more will come. I can't protect her by myself, and I'm not ready to go through official channels. Not until I know more about what I'm dealing with."

Cole was still on medical leave after being shot in the shoulder during another case. He was nearly healed and would be back to full duty in the next couple of weeks. Until then, he was sidelined. Which was why Daniel called him.

"I'll understand if you say no, but if you're willing, I could use the backup."

Cole was silent for a long moment. "Do you trust her?"

Daniel didn't answer right away. He knew exactly what Cole meant. She was lying to them—or at least, she wasn't saying everything she knew—but was her heart in the right place? Was she someone he could put his faith in?

Just then, another toddler wandered into the play area. Ellie welcomed the child with a warm smile and offered her a block. Within moments, the little girl had climbed into Ellie's lap beside Owen. Ellie wrapped her arms around both kids and kept chatting, gently placing another block atop the newly built tower.

Unexpected emotion tightened Daniel's throat. He'd seen the worst humanity had to offer. His instincts were sharp, his trust hard-earned, but Ellie made something inside him soften. Something he didn't know still existed.

"Yes," he said quietly. "I trust her."

"Then I'll be at your ranch by dinnertime. Word of warning though. If I get injured while helping you out, you're the one who has to explain it to Olivia. According to her, bandages don't go with my tux."

Daniel laughed. Olivia Leighton was Cole's fiancée. Their wedding was in a few weeks, right before he returned to full duty. "I'll bubble wrap you before the bad guys arrive. And Cole... thanks."

"You're welcome. See you soon."

He hung up and rose from the chair, intending to join Ellie and the children in their block-building activity, when a nurse called out Owen's name. She led them to a small exam room. For the next half hour, Owen was poked and prodded before being deemed healthy by his pediatric cardiologist.

Seeing Owen's scar for the first time was still a shock. Daniel knew he'd had surgery, but the thick strip of healed tissue running down the little boy's chest was evidence of just how invasive the procedure had been.

Ellie handled the entire visit with ease. She spoke medical jargon as if she had a degree herself. Once again, Daniel was struck by just how tough Ellie was. She didn't flinch when things got hard. She dealt with it. Adapted. Learned and kept moving forward.

It was impressive, and it made him wonder what steps Ellie had taken to handle the current danger. Who had she called? Her superiors? A trusted friend? He knew she was waiting for a phone call from someone. Daniel had spotted the burner phone tucked behind an extra packet of wipes in the diaper bag. It hadn't been there yesterday.

Ellie snapped the last button on Owen's shirt and then lifted him from the exam table. "Okay. Good to go." She glanced at her watch. "We have 40 minutes to get home before lunch and naptime, or there'll be a melt-down. Think you can get us home in time?"

Daniel smiled. "I'll do my best." He tossed the diaper bag over his shoulder and escorted Ellie back to the waiting room. She needed to sign some papers at the front desk, so he took Owen. The little boy patted Daniel's cheek with a slightly wet hand and cuddled Scout. Daniel play-acted like he was going to nibble on the tiny fingers creeping toward his mouth, even as his gaze roamed the waiting room.

Everything appeared normal. Still, he wouldn't let his guard down until they were all safely back on the ranch.

Owen giggled. The laugh was infectious, and despite his efforts to stay alert, Daniel found himself chuckling too. And when Owen laid his head down on Daniel's chest, a pang of longing and grief struck him so sudden and fierce, it nearly buckled his knees.

He hadn't let himself think about the baby he lost. Not in years.

His ex-wife had miscarried at five months. The loss hadn't destroyed their marriage—it was already crumbling—but it delivered the final blow. Divorce followed. The combined tragedy had scarred Daniel's heart in a way that couldn't be repaired. He hadn't dated since. Not in a decade. Why bother? He had no intention of ever remarrying. Once had been enough.

"Earth to Daniel." Ellie waved a hand in front of his face.

He blinked, jolted straight out of his thoughts. Belatedly, he realized she'd been calling his name.

"Are you okay?" Her brows furrowed. "You look upset."

"I'm fine." His tone was gruff, but he was irritated to have lost focus. And he absolutely did not want to talk about his failed marriage or the reason his throat had thickened with tears. "Ready to go?"

"Yep." She held out her hands. "I'll take Owen."

"I've got him." Daniel might not want to talk about the baby he'd lost, but he wasn't ready to relinquish the one in his arms just yet. Owen's head was still nestled against his chest, his fingers absently playing with the buttons on Daniel's shirt. He wanted to savor the feeling a bit longer.

"Uh-oh," Ellie teased as they exited the doctor's office into the hallway. "You've fallen victim."

"Excuse me?"

"That little guy has just about everyone in Silver Creek wrapped around his finger. You should see how the ladies of the sewing circle fight over him. I have to practically wrestle him away from them in order to take him home." Her lips curled into a soft smile. "Seems like Owen worked his magic on you too. Like I said, another victim."

Daniel slanted a glance her way. "What happens when he screams like he did during the exam? I'm sure the ladies of the sewing circle are happy to give him back when he gets grumpy."

She laughed. "You'd think so, but nope. They just rush to do his bidding. He's going to be spoiled rotten if I don't find a way to..." Her voice trailed off as a pained look crossed her face. "Never mind."

"No, finish the thought."

Ellie stayed quiet. And suddenly, Daniel understood exactly what she was waiting for. He halted midstep, drawing her to a stop beside him. "You called for an extraction, didn't you? For you and Owen."

"How did—"

"I saw the cell phone." His mind whirled. The cell phone was still in the bag. The same bag slung over his shoulder. "Who did you call, Ellie?" His gaze fixed on her intently, his tone demanding. "Who?"

The elevator dinged and then swooshed open. The movement caught Daniel's attention. Two men exited wearing scrubs. His pulse spiked as he noticed their medical masks and dirty boots. Not doctors. Not nurses.

"We have to move." Daniel wrapped an arm around Ellie's shoulders and turned her away from the men. His voice was pitched low to keep it from carrying as they traversed the long hallway. "The stairwell. Hurry."

With luck, they'd escape before the men spotted them.

To her credit, Ellie didn't ask questions. Her complexion pale, her steps quick, she kept pace alongside him. A family spilled out of a nearby doctor's office, their loud voices reverberating down the hall. Daniel kept going. The weight of Owen in his arms added pressure to the moment. It also complicated things. He couldn't pull his weapon.

Five more steps and they'd be at the stairwell. Ellie lengthened her stride and reached the door first. She yanked it open. Daniel risked one glance back.

And made direct eye contact with one of the masked men as he pulled a small handgun from the pocket of his scrubs.

"Run!" Daniel ducked into the stairwell and raced down the first flight of stairs behind Ellie. Her braid flew behind her as she bounded down the stairs.

Feet pounded above them. The attackers were coming.

Adrenaline surged through Daniel as he kept pace with Ellie. The diaper bag bounced against his back and Owen, jostled by their sudden dash down several flights of stairs, wailed. His screams covered the sound of the approaching men, but Daniel knew there wasn't a moment to waste. Chest heaving, he burst onto the ground floor of the hospital. The stairwell opened into the ER lobby.

"Which way?" Ellie gasped.

It was a good question. They needed to escape, but there was no way of knowing if another set of attackers waited at the car. He considered their options in half a heartbeat. "Into the emergency room."

Ellie didn't hesitate. She pivoted on her heel and raced ahead. Owen's screams attracted attention, and Daniel wanted to comfort him, but there was no time. The stairwell door crashed open behind him. Gasps followed as the men spilled into the waiting room. Daniel didn't waste time looking back.

Please, Lord, let this plan work.

Clutching Owen to his chest, Daniel pushed through the swinging doors into the emergency wing. A security guard had already stopped Ellie, and another moved to intercept him. Daniel shifted Owen to reveal the ranger badge pinned to his chest. "I'm law enforcement. She's with me. Two men dressed in scrubs and masks are chasing us. They have guns."

Before either security guard could ask more questions, Daniel grabbed Ellie's hand and pulled her farther into the emergency room. They weaved around doctors and patients crowding the hallways. He turned a corner and found a break room. Ducking inside, he acted quickly, handing Owen over to Ellie and then removing the burner phone from the diaper bag, along with her personal one. "Give me your smart watch."

All the devices could be used to track them. Daniel

suspected that whoever Ellie had called for rescue was not a friend to her.

Panting from exertion, she paused in comforting Owen to rip the watch from her wrist. He smashed all the devices before dumping them in the trash can. Then he peered cautiously out into the hallway. Voices carried. Angry ones. As Daniel had hoped, the security guards intercepted the men chasing them.

But this wasn't over.

Not by a long shot.

EIGHT

Things had gone from bad to worse.

Ellie cupped her hands under the bathroom faucet and splashed cold water on her face. Droplets raced down her cheeks and dripped off her chin. She grabbed a few paper towels and patted her face dry, then pressed them to the back of her neck, which was slick with sweat from their frantic escape through the hospital.

If only washing away her mistakes were that simple.

A shiver raced down her spine. If those men at the hospital had caught them, Daniel would've been killed. Owen, taken. And she would be left floundering, still completely in the dark about what they were searching for.

How had they traced her to the hospital? Through her personal phone? Or the burner she'd used to contact the FBI?

The taste of betrayal was bitter on her tongue.

The Iron Fist had moles in law enforcement. It was

one of the reasons the FBI had changed her identity outside the normal channels. Still, she'd never believed someone from her own department would turn on her. And now... now she couldn't shake the fear that someone inside the Bureau had sold her out. If that was true, she was alone. With Owen to protect.

A terrifying thought.

She stared at her reflection in the mirror. The stress had aged her overnight. Her complexion was pale, her cheekbones sharp with fatigue. She wasn't foolish enough to think she could take on a powerful criminal network by herself. Nor could she leave Owen. He was hers in every way that mattered, except by blood or legal decree. She'd filed for adoption six months ago. The paperwork wasn't completed yet, but if these threats continued, it never would be.

There was one Hail Mary left.

Ellie stepped from the bathroom into the hallway. The low murmur of voices in the Silver Creek Police Department bullpen offered a small measure of reassurance. They were safe for the moment. Daniel had brought them straight here after the hospital attack to debrief Chief O'Neal. The men were in the chief's office with Owen.

She had a few minutes at most.

Hurrying past the chief's office, she entered the break room. A wall phone rested on the counter beside the coffee machine. Ellie moved quickly, dialing a number she knew by heart.

"Federal Bureau of Investigation, Austin Field Office. How may I direct your call?"

Ellie gripped the receiver. "Special Agent in Charge, James Callahan."

Clicking followed. Then the operator came back on, still cheerful. "I'm sorry, ma'am, but Special Agent Callahan is retired. Is there someone else I can connect you to?"

Her stomach dropped. Retired. Just like that, her last hope vanished. There was no one she trusted more than Callahan. She swallowed hard. "No. I need to speak with Callahan. Do you have a number where he can be reached? Or a way to get him a message?"

"I'm sorry, ma'am. I don't. Would you like—"

She hung up, the click of the receiver like a death knell. Her entire body felt both numb and cold.

"Ellie."

Daniel's voice sent her pulse skyrocketing. She jumped, releasing her grip on the phone receiver as guilt flooded through her. She wasn't supposed to be in here. And the last phone call she'd made had likely put them in danger. Two facts Daniel was well aware of.

His dark eyes moved from her to the phone and back again. Disappointment flickered across his face, and his expression hardened. "We have a problem. Owen's caseworker is here. She needs to speak to you."

A wave of unease crashed over Ellie as she followed him into Chief O'Neal's office. Owen's caseworker, Maggie Lyons, stood in the center of the room with her hands on her hips. The older woman had graying brown hair, reading glasses on a chain around her neck, and a permanent furrow between her brows. Ellie and Maggie had always gotten along well, but judging from her scowl, Maggie was furious.

Roy bounced Owen on his knee, but his expression was grave. "This is a mistake, Maggie, and you know it."

"What's going on?" Ellie's heart began to pound.

"It's come to my attention there have been threatening incidents. I had to drive here for a full report." Maggie's tone was clipped. "Information that should have come from you."

With everything going on, Ellie hadn't even thought to call Owen's caseworker. "I'm sorry—"

"Too little, too late. Now that I've been fully informed by Chief O'Neal, it's too dangerous to leave Owen in your care. I'm placing him in a new foster home for his protection."

"You can't." Ellie couldn't keep the panic from her voice. She crossed the room and gently took Owen from Roy's arms. The little boy clung to her neck, and the tears that sprang to her eyes were instant. "Moving Owen won't necessarily protect him, and it'll be scary and confusing for him. His health is still fragile, and he's never known another caregiver. Taking him away would be a terrible mistake." Ellie listed every reason they shouldn't be separated. "I've filed for adoption. It'll be final in a few months."

For a second, Maggie's expression softened. Then her mouth set with resolve. "But it isn't final yet. Until then, Owen is a ward of the state, and it's my responsibility to ensure his safety. The chief and I have discussed the best course of action. Owen's new placement will be kept secret. He'll be perfectly safe."

Ellie looked desperately at Roy, but he seemed as stricken as she felt. She had no legal standing to stop this. Her throat closed as panic threatened to swallow her. She hugged Owen tighter, blinking back the tears that threatened to fall.

"What about you?" Daniel's voice was calm, almost casual. But his attention was fixed on Maggie. "Who's going to keep you safe?"

Maggie blinked. "Excuse me?"

"You'll know where Owen is. The men hunting Ellie and Owen were bold enough to attack in a hospital. We don't know who they are or what they want. Do you really think they wouldn't come after you to find him?"

Ellie's breath caught. Her gaze darted to Daniel, but his focus stayed on Maggie. The caseworker had gone pale.

Roy's head snapped up, and his eyes narrowed appreciatively. "Daniel has a point, Maggie. What do you propose?"

Daniel shifted his weight. "The wisest course of action is to keep Owen and Ellie together. They're staying on my ranch, under my protection. I've already called another member of my ranger team to assist, and if need be, I can ask for more help. No one will get close to Owen. That I can assure you." Now his gaze shifted to the baby before lifting to meet Ellie's. "It's my duty to protect him and I take that job very seriously."

Her heart swelled with gratitude. Daniel had every reason to be angry with her. Every reason to doubt her. This was his opportunity to step forward and explain that Ellie was lying about her identity, to share that it was her actions that'd placed Owen in danger. Instead, he'd chosen to protect her, as he'd done from the first moment they met.

He was a good man. A very good man.

"I'll have patrol officers do periodic check-ins at the ranch," Roy added. "The sheriff can pitch in with a few deputies as well. Frequent rounds at the ranch should deter anyone from attempting an attack."

"I also have a top-of-the-line security system at the ranch. And trusted workers who keep an eye on the property," Daniel said. "The safest place for Owen is with me."

Maggie was quiet for a long moment, her furrow deepening. Then she sighed. "Fine, but I reserve the right to change my mind if I think Owen's safety is at risk. Surprise visits will also happen." She fixed Daniel with a hard stare. "You're not the only one who takes their job seriously."

If Daniel was offended by her jab, no sign of it showed in his expression. Instead, he nodded respectfully. "Yes, ma'am."

Maggie collected her purse. "Miss Brooks. Chief O'Neal. I expect to be updated on this matter regularly."

Ellie nodded her agreement, not trusting her voice. Owen babbled and played with strands of her hair. His sweet, lilting voice was music to her ears. She pressed a kiss to his curls and sent up a prayer of thanksgiving. Crisis after crisis had hit, but she and Owen were still together.

But for how long? And how could Ellie ensure her baby's safety?

The problems plaguing her weighed down her shoulders and slowed her steps as Daniel escorted her from the police department to his Explorer. Ellie loaded Owen into his car seat, handing him Scout to play with. Daniel stood guard. His eyes swept the surrounding area, scanning for trouble. Rough stubble lined his jaw, and his hat threw shadows across his features, but his watchful presence was comforting, not overwhelming.

Gratitude washed over her yet again. Ellie placed a hand on his chest. "Thank you. For what you did in the chief's office."

"I told the truth. The safest place for Owen is on my ranch."

She nodded and was about to drop her hand when he covered it with his own, holding it in place. "Ellie..." His jaw clenched briefly, and then he sighed, long and low. "I wasn't completely honest. Yes, Owen is safer on my ranch, but I wanted you to stay together. You love him as if he's your own. That's no small gift. He needs you. You need each other."

Her throat tightened. She shouldn't lean on him. Couldn't. But her body moved before her mind caught up, seeking the only solid thing in her crumbling world. Ellie wrapped her arms around Daniel's waist.

He embraced her without hesitation, surrounding her

with warmth and strength. She drew in her first deep breath since the hospital attack. The scent of his cedar cologne filled her lungs, clean and woodsy, like the outdoors. It was grounding. Comforting. In a way she couldn't explain.

"We're at a crossroads here, Ellie." His tone was soft and caring. "The way I see it, you're in deep trouble. Whoever you've called on to help may have betrayed you. You need to trust someone. Let it be me."

Heaven help her, she wanted to. So much.

"What if the truth puts you in a position where you have to lie? What if it means putting your badge at risk?" She lifted her gaze to his. "Do you still want it?"

He scanned her expression for a moment, as if gauging how serious she was. Whatever he saw there had his gaze drifting to Owen before returning to her. His brown eyes turned steely with determination. "If it means being able to keep you both safe, then yes, I still want it."

NINE

He was in deep, there was no doubt about it.

Daniel pushed against the rocking chair on the enclosed porch and sipped his iced tea. The book his mother had bought him for Christmas rested on the wicker coffee table in front of him. *Murder on the Banks.* One of Ellie's books, though she published under a pseudonym.

That thought made him snort. Ellie Brooks wasn't even her real name.

It was a strange feeling. To be so drawn to someone whose true identity he didn't even know. Dangerous too. He'd been burned before. Ellie wasn't his ex-wife, not at all, but the pattern remained the same.

Complicated women. They were his type.

Voices filtered from the kitchen. Cole had arrived two hours ago and promptly made himself useful by eating them out of house and home. Daniel glanced through the screen door and caught sight of his friend plowing through a slice of cherry pie. Unbelievable. How did he have room for it all?

Cole said something too low to catch, and Marta laughed in reply. She'd always liked Cole. Or maybe, like Daniel, she appreciated having another lawman on the premises.

Daniel set his empty glass down and picked up the hardback. It had been published last year and featured a police officer tracking a serial killer. The review quotes on the cover called it "thrilling" and "well-researched." The author bio didn't include a photo and was vague enough to protect Ellie's identity. Smart. It was unlikely the men hunting her had located her through her books.

The screen door creaked. Ellie stepped onto the porch in an oversized hoodie and jeans, her hair falling in soft waves over her shoulders. She looked tired. Tense.

She crossed to the railing and breathed in deep. "It's so pretty here. Peaceful."

"It is. Owen go down okay?"

"He didn't last through story time. Missing his nap really threw off his afternoon." She turned to face him. "Putting him to bed this early risks a middle-of-the-night wakeup, but after his third meltdown, I figured he'd had enough."

Ellie probably had too. Daniel hated to put her through a difficult conversation, but it needed to be done. He set the book back on the table and stood. There were about two more hours of sunlight left. Enough for a nearby stroll. "Want to see my favorite spot on the ranch?"

Her brow furrowed slightly, and then she nodded. Daniel took her hand. Her skin was soft, the brush of her palm against his sending a jolt of attraction straight to his heart. He ignored it, leading her off the porch and onto a pathway that curved around the house. Beyond the last fence post, the land opened into a narrow trail shaded by oaks. Wildflowers brushed their jeans as they moved between the trees. He knew this path by heart, could walk it even in the dark.

Soon the faint sound of trickling water reached his ears. The creek bent in a gentle curve, the water catching the light in golden ripples. A few smooth boulders flanked the bank, and a weathered bench rested beneath an old pecan tree, half-shadowed by the overhang of leaves.

Ellie's eyes widened. Her lips curved into a smile that nearly stole his breath. "Wow, you weren't kidding. This is beautiful."

"It was my hiding spot as a kid." He gave her hand a gentle squeeze, then let go.

"What were you hiding from?"

"I have six brothers and sisters. I was hiding from everyone."

She chuckled. "I was an only child. My best friend, Lisa, lived next door and had three siblings. Two brothers and a younger sister. I came up with every excuse under the sun to hang out with them. The house was chaos and always loud, and there was a mess everywhere, but it was also warm and fun. Her mom baked all the time. To this day, the smell of chocolate chip cookies reminds me of a loving home."

He cocked his head sideways, studying her. "Was it so different from your own house?"

"Night and day. My parents were professors. Bookish and introverted. No one ever raised their voice or played practical jokes. Don't get me wrong, Mom and Dad loved me, but their idea of a good time was a documentary, not a midnight swim at the lake." She glanced at Daniel. "I guess, in the end, we always want what we don't have. You longed for quiet. I wanted lively."

He leaned one shoulder against the pecan tree. "Where are they now? Your folks, I mean."

"Deceased. A car accident when I was in college." She sighed. "Not everything I told people is a lie."

"Must be hard. Keeping your story straight, facts mixed with falsehoods."

She scoffed. "I'm a pro." Ellie tucked her hands into the pocket of her hoodie. "My real name is Elizabeth Conway. Three years ago, I was a Special Agent with the FBI working undercover to infiltrate a white supremacist organization known as the Iron Fist."

Daniel stiffened, his shoulders drawing back. He wasn't surprised to learn Ellie was an FBI Agent—he'd already deduced she was in law enforcement—but the Iron Fist connection ratcheted up the danger several notches. The gang started in Austin but had expanded their operations to Houston and San Antonio. They trafficked in drugs, illegal weapons, and people.

They were also known for their brutality. Murder

and mutilation were the tip of the iceberg. The Texas Rangers took part in several active investigations connected to the gang, but so far, had been unable to dismantle the operation.

"How long were you undercover?" he asked.

"Two years. My mission was two-fold: identify the leader of the Iron Fist and obtain enough evidence to bring down the entire network. It took time, but I climbed into the upper ranks of the group and discovered that Gideon Voss was the leader."

Daniel stared at her. "Gideon Voss? The business-man?" His mind whirled. Gideon had risen to fame by building a tech company and was well-connected to several powerful politicians. "Are you sure?"

Ellie gave a sharp nod, her voice like ice. "Gideon owns legitimate businesses and uses them to mask his illegal ones. Money and power are his drugs of choice. He also deeply believes in the white supremacy ideology, which is obvious once you dig into his social media posts. Problem is, he's also incredibly suspicious. He controls the Iron Fist through a hand-selected network of lieu-tenants who are extremely loyal. It's nearly impossible to breach their inner circle."

Daniel leveled a glance her way. "Something tells me you still found a way in."

A ghost of a smile touched her lips before fading. "I befriended Gideon's mistress, Lena Grainger." Ellie crossed to the bench under the tree and sat. "Lena was eighteen when she met Gideon. He groomed her, abused her. By the time we met, Lena was twenty-five and desperate to escape. I flipped her. Convinced Lena that if she turned over evidence that led to Gideon's arrest, the FBI would give her immunity for her crimes and a ticket to a new life."

She drew in a breath and let it out slowly. "She was smart, Daniel. An experienced hacker and a mathematical genius. Slowly, Lena started feeding me information. Good information. The FBI was able to take down several big fish in the Iron Fist. But she was terrified of turning on Gideon. She was convinced that even with a new identity he'd find her."

Daniel heard the emotion in her voice. "You cared about her."

Ellie nodded. "I did. When she called out of the blue and said she had the final piece—the thing that would bring Gideon down—I knew she'd finally had enough. She texted me a location."

"You went alone?"

"We'd done it before. There wasn't time to loop in my handler, and I trusted her." She shook her head. "I should have been more careful."

Daniel braced himself. "What happened?"

"The meeting point was an abandoned warehouse. When I arrived, I discovered Lena. Murdered. Before I could get out of there, an unknown assailant shot me." Ellie removed her hands from the pockets of her hoodie and shifted the fabric, along with the shirt underneath, until a stretch of mottled skin on her abdomen was visible.

Gunshot wounds. The scars had faded to a dull

white, but the starkness of the injury against her other-wise flawless skin ignited a wave of fury in him.

"I nearly died." Ellie dropped her shirt and hoodie back into place. "A couple of homeless people found me bleeding out and called 911. By the time I woke up in the hospital, the Iron Fist had a hit out on me. Whatever evidence Lena had collected was lost. There was no way to take Gideon down. It was decided the best course of action was to make everyone—including the Iron Fist—believe I'd died that day. So Elizabeth Conway died, and Ellie Brooks was born."

Daniel joined her on the bench. Dragonflies skirted along the edge of the creek before flitting off into the trees. It was a lot to process, and he had so many questions. "When the attack at the church happened, did you suspect the Iron Fist was involved?"

"No. I genuinely believed Owen was the target. It was only after we discovered my house had been broken into and searched that I realized they'd found me."

"Do you know what they're looking for?"

She shook her head emphatically. "Not a clue. I was being honest about that."

"Could it be the evidence Lena collected?"

"I suppose it's possible, but it doesn't make much sense. If I had it, I would've handed it over to the FBI a long time ago. Plus, the Iron Fist wouldn't want the evidence found. They'd be more likely to kill me than to ask me to find it."

All good points. Daniel put a pin in that for the

moment. He turned to face her. "The burner phone. You used it to call the FBI, didn't you?"

"Yes. I was given an emergency number to call in case my identity was ever compromised. No one answered. No one called back. I left several messages." Her hands knotted together in her lap. "The Iron Fist is rumored to have moles inside of several federal agencies. Based on the fact that we were attacked at the hospital, coupled with the lack of response to my emergency calls, I think it's safe to say someone in the FBI ratted me out."

He agreed with that assessment. "And the phone call at the police station?"

"I was trying to reach my old boss, James Callahan, but he's retired now. He's one of the few people I trusted." Her gaze grew distant. "I was betrayed. Twice. Somehow Gideon found out about my meeting with Lena, and I doubt it was from her."

"Someone on your team leaked it."

She jerked her head in agreement. "It's the only logical conclusion."

Daniel frowned. "Wouldn't the mole have leaked your new identity earlier?"

"Probably. But only a handful of people knew I survived. My FBI file was sealed. Everyone else—my team, the Bureau, even my handler—believes I'm dead. That my cover lasted this long means the Iron Fist must've found me some other way."

"But you don't know how."

"No." Ellie hesitated and then reached out to touch his arm. "I'm sorry, Daniel. I wanted to tell you everything earlier, but I was ordered to maintain my cover at all costs. There are protocols when things go wrong... Following them put you in danger." She pressed her lips together as if to contain some runaway emotion. "I screwed up."

"No, Ellie." He took her hand and squeezed it gently. "There's nothing to apologize for. You did what you were ordered to do by people you trust. Now, given all that's happened, we need to figure out a way to keep you and Owen safe."

A determined look settled over her features. "The only way to keep Owen safe is by finding whatever the Iron Fist thinks I have and either destroying it or getting it into the right hands." She pulled her hand from his and stood. "Which is exactly what I intend to do."

He rose. "Not on your own."

"No, Daniel. I can't ask you to help me beyond keeping Owen safe." A stubborn tilt jutted her chin up. "As it stands now, you're compromised. Don't you get it? This is an FBI case. Legally and technically, you're supposed to loop them in. By not doing so, you're putting your badge at risk."

"I have no intention of risking my badge or informing the FBI about our investigation." Daniel placed his hands gently on her shoulders before she could make a run for it. "I know you're scared, Ellie, and you have every right to be, but we can't take on the Iron Fist on our own. My superior, Lieutenant Rodriguez, can be trusted. She may keep the team small and on a need-to-know basis, but she won't put either you or Owen's life at risk. I guarantee it."

Ellie hesitated and then gave a small nod. "Okay."

It wasn't full trust—but it was something. And given the betrayals she'd endured, Daniel knew it meant everything.

He pulled her into his arms. She didn't resist. Her head rested against his chest, and slowly, her rigid posture relaxed beneath his touch. The rippling of the creek as it weaved around the rocks created a soothing backdrop. The setting sun hadn't left the sky, but the shadows under the pecan tree had deepened. They needed to head back to the house soon.

But not yet.

Daniel held her closer. The silky strands of her hair tickled his chin, the scent of her shampoo filling his senses. She was so delicate next to him, but there was an iron rod of steel running through her. There had to be. Ellie was a survivor. She'd lost her home, her career, nearly her life. Instead of curling up into a ball of anger, she'd started fresh. Made friends. Built a career. Taken on a sick child.

He wanted to shield her from everything that came next. The urge was potent and overwhelming, and unlike anything he'd ever experienced before. But Daniel was wise enough to know his limitations.

He couldn't guarantee safety or answers. But he could make her one promise.

She wouldn't face it alone.

TEN

Wind whispered through the leaves and sunlight dappled the grass as Ellie pushed Owen in the baby swing hanging from an old oak tree. His giggles warmed her heart but couldn't erase the nerves jangling through her.

After their conversation by the creek, Daniel informed his boss about the situation. This afternoon, Lieutenant Vikki Rodriguez arrived with another ranger, Jonah Foster. Daniel and his colleague Cole were with them in the dining room.

They were talking. About her. About the threats against her and Owen.

Ellie wanted to be a part of the conversation, but she was no longer an FBI Agent. Some things had to be discussed outside of her purview. Not an easy pill to swallow. Especially now when her life was spinning out of control. Could she trust Daniel to be her port in the storm? To advocate for her and Owen's best interests?

She'd only known him a few days. And yet... inexplicably something deep inside her whispered yes. Yes, she could trust him.

"If you keep biting that lip, it's going to bleed." Marta's tone was gentle, but concern darkened her chestnut-colored eyes. She handed Ellie a glass of iced tea and motioned toward the bench under the oak. "Sit, mamasita. I'll push Owen."

Ellie released her bottom lip and took a long sip of the sweet iced tea. The cold glass against her mouth soothed the sting. She hadn't even realized she'd been gnawing at it. A sign of just how worried she was.

Marta gave Owen a push, and he giggled wildly, curls bouncing in the breeze. Scout was nestled beside him in the seat, his floppy ears waving with the motion. Jinx snoozed on the grass next to the bench. The dog opened one eye as Ellie sat, then rolled over with a sigh of contentment.

Ellie traced her fingers along the smooth wooden armrest. "Did your husband make this?"

"Yes." Marta seemed pleased that Ellie recognized her late husband's handiwork. "Sam built it so we could watch our grandkids play in the yard." Her smile faltered as sadness crept in.

Ellie didn't need her to explain. Sam had passed away a few years back after only a short time with his grandchildren. "You must miss him."

"Every day. We had forty-five years together. Some hard, some easy, but always full of love."

The warmth in Marta's tone tugged at Ellie's long-buried dreams. There'd been a time she'd wanted a husband to share her life with and a house full of kids. But her career had come first. She'd thought there'd be time for everything else. And now...

She rotated the glass in her hands. "It's hard to imagine spending forty-five years with one person. I've changed so much, I'm not sure I recognize the woman I used to be." Ellie let her attention drift across the pastures dotted with horses. "I was fearless and stubborn."

Marta let out an unladylike snort. "What makes you think you're not fearless and stubborn now?" She scooped Owen up, who was starting to fuss, and joined Ellie on the bench. Her voice softened. "I won't pretend to know what's going on, mamasita, but you have a warrior's spirit. Motherhood may have softened you, opened your heart maybe, but it hasn't changed your grit and determination. Don't doubt yourself."

She was full of doubts. Had been since the first attack.

Ellie brushed her thumb over Owen's chubby hand. "I have more to lose now."

"That may be, but you're much stronger than you know." Marta smiled gently. "God will see you through."

Her words brought comfort to Ellie's troubled heart. She'd spent so long trying to survive, trying to shield Owen from every threat, that she'd forgotten what it meant to lean on her faith. To trust that God had a plan.

The screen door creaked open. Daniel stepped onto the porch. Sunlight caught his dark hair and outlined his broad shoulders. The memory of being held in his arms last night flashed unbidden in Ellie's mind. Heat bloomed in her cheeks.

Foolish. Dangerous. Developing feelings for Daniel would only make things messier. But the ache in her chest refused to be ignored. He made her feel safe. And Ellie couldn't remember the last time she truly felt that way.

His eyes found hers, and the warmth in them made her pulse skip. "Ellie, we're ready for you."

Marta gave her knee a gentle pat. Ellie kissed Owen before following Daniel inside. The house smelled of cinnamon and coffee. Voices filtered from the kitchen, but Daniel led her to the dining room.

Lieutenant Vikki Rodriguez stood at the window. She turned as they entered, her expression unreadable, but a small smile curved her lips. "Sorry to keep you waiting, Miss Brooks. There were a few housekeeping matters we needed to take care of."

"Please call me Ellie."

She nodded and gestured to a seat nearby. "Daniel has brought me up to date regarding the delicate situation we find ourselves in. I want to start off by reassuring you that no one on this team, including myself, will contact the FBI about this case until we can be certain that doing so won't endanger you and Owen." Her eyes darkened with bridled fury. "If there is a mole in the Bureau, we'll root him out."

Ellie appreciated the lieutenant's confidence, but her conscience pricked. "Thank you, Lieutenant. And I don't want to sound ungrateful, but when the FBI finds out you didn't call them... they won't be pleased. They may pressure your superiors to launch an investigation that could land you all in trouble."

"I know how to protect my team." Lieutenant Rodriguez arched her brow. "Besides, I don't know who you are. I only know who you *claim* to be."

Smart. Very smart. Ellie couldn't help the smile tugging at her lips. "I suppose without DNA or fingerprints, it's impossible to know if I am Agent Elizabeth Conway."

Vikki smiled back. "Precisely. And we have no physical evidence linking the Iron Fist to the attacks. No IDs on the men from the church or the hospital. As far as I'm concerned, there's no need to alert the FBI. Yet." She leveled a look toward Ellie. "If that changes, I'll be sure to let you know."

"Understood." Gratitude swelled. "Thank you, Lieutenant."

"No need to thank me, Ellie. I'm just doing my job." She paused and her tone softened. "We've all made enemies in this line of work, and we take care of our own. I'm sorry the past has come back to haunt you. We'll do everything in our power to keep you and Owen safe."

Relief uncoiled the last knot of fear twisting her stomach. Daniel had been right. His boss was formidable and trustworthy.

Vikki rose and picked up her coffee mug. "I'm going to bring in the rest of the team. While I'm in the kitchen, I'm grabbing another homemade cinnamon roll. Can I get something for either of you?"

Both shook their heads. After she left, Daniel angled his body toward Ellie. His expression was slightly guarded, as if he was concerned she'd regret trusting him. "What do you think?"

"I'm glad I listened to you." Ellie reached for his hand. "Thank you. For the first time since this started, I feel like I can breathe."

He interlaced their fingers and gently squeezed her hand before lifting his gaze to meet hers. "So I won't wake up one morning to discover you disappeared with Owen?"

She inhaled sharply. Ellie shouldn't have been surprised by the question. Daniel was intuitive, and the thought had crossed her mind more than once last night, but she was caught off-guard by the emotion in his voice. Worry. For her? Or for Owen? Ellie wasn't sure.

His brows rose. "Shocked I figured it out? You're not as subtle as you think."

"Obviously." There'd been a time, while working undercover, when Ellie had been excellent at hiding her thoughts and emotions. Those skills had clearly faded since living in Silver Creek. She licked her lips. "I won't lie. It's crossed my mind. But a life on the run wouldn't be fair to Owen. I would never do that to him if there was another way. Besides, I'm not sure I can keep him safe by myself." Ellie paused. "And before you ask, no, I won't go rogue and take on the Iron Fist by myself or try to find whatever they're looking for on my own. I'll play by the rules the lieutenant lays out."

Daniel's lips quirked up in a teasing smile. "Oof. That hurt to say, didn't it?"

She lightly smacked his shoulder. "Don't make fun. Why do you care, anyway? We hardly know each other. I'm surprised you aren't looking to get rid of me and the trouble I've brought to your doorstep."

"You couldn't be more wrong."

Daniel leaned forward slightly, his expression serious and intent. The space between them seemed to shrink, and Ellie found herself holding her breath. His eyes searched hers with an intensity that made her pulse quicken.

"I care. You're right that we hardly know each other, but I can see the kind of person you are. Someone who'd risk everything for that little boy. You're also used to working undercover, adapting to the situation, and calling the shots if need be. But that won't work this time. We're doing this as a team. No more secrets. No more lies. I need your word, El."

El. For Ellie. And for Elizabeth. Daniel chose a nickname that encompassed both parts of her. It sent her heart spinning. As illogical as it was, given the amount of time they'd known each other, he understood her. It was both comforting and terrifying in equal measure.

She nodded slowly. "I promise. No more secrets or lies." Ellie met his eyes steadily. "But I expect the same from you."

Building real trust would require honesty on both sides, especially after what she'd been through. She couldn't afford to be blindsided again by someone keeping secrets.

Daniel hesitated, then nodded decisively. "Complete honesty. You have my word." He stepped back, creating some professional distance between them. "Starting now."

Her pulse jumped. "What did you find out?"

"We know how the Iron Fist found you. More importantly, we know what they're looking for."

Ellie opened her mouth, but before she could voice a question, an alarm on Daniel's phone blared. He shot out of his seat, his attention jerking to the window. Ellie jumped up too. Her gaze followed his to the yard where Marta and Owen were playing in the grass.

She grabbed Daniel's arm. "What is it?"

He was already moving to the door. "We need to get Owen inside. Someone's breached the ranch security system."

ELEVEN

Fifteen minutes later, Daniel stood in front of the television in the living room, watching grainy footage from his property's security system. Two men in camouflage and ball caps slipped onto the north side of his property. They carried assault rifles. Moments later, ranch hands spotted them. Shots were exchanged. Then the intruders bolted for the road, escaping in an SUV with mud-caked license plates.

Daniel's grip tightened on the remote. No one had been hurt, thank God, but things could've gone very differently.

"It's either very stupid or very cocky to trespass onto a Texas Ranger's land in broad daylight," Cole drawled. He was draped over an armchair, and despite the casual tone and posture, a thread of anger ran through his voice. "Honestly, forget the Texas Ranger part. Ranch hands in Texas carry guns. Those must be city boys."

"They're the same men who attacked us at the hospital," Ellie added, rocking Owen gently in her arms. The little boy's eyes were drifting shut. "Not terribly smart. Sloppy too. That's unusual for the Iron Fist. They're more strategic. More careful."

"Supports our theory." Texas Ranger Jonah Foster rocked on his heels. He resembled a Viking with his broad stature and light coloring—all that was missing was the beard. No one looking at him would ever think he was a computer wizard and dark web expert. Until he opened his mouth. He'd put Daniel to sleep more than once talking about cryptocurrency and IP masking through virtual tunnels.

"What theory?" Ellie's eyes narrowed.

Daniel took Owen from her arms and cradled him against his chest. "Jonah thinks the men who are after you aren't working for the Iron Fist."

Her eyes widened. "What?"

"There was a split about six months ago," Jonah explained. "One of the Iron Fist's lieutenants, Tobias Kincaid, broke off from the group and took a handful of men with him. He carved out a section of the business and set up his own operation. Since then, there have been skirmishes between the two groups. The Rangers confirmed Gideon Voss leads the Iron Fist during a murder investigation last year, but there still isn't enough direct evidence to arrest him. Tobias wants that to change. He wants Gideon out of the way so he can take control of the Iron Fist."

Ellie sank onto the couch. "He's looking for the evidence Lena stole."

"Yes." Daniel tucked Owen into the playpen and draped a lightweight blanket over him before turning to face Ellie. His heart stuttered. What was it about this woman that unmoored him? No matter how much he tried to ignore his growing attraction, it kept hitting him at the worst times.

Falling for Ellie would be a terrible mistake. The last time he'd run with his emotions instead of logic, the relationship ended in a bitter divorce. That wasn't a failure he intended to repeat. Ellie was skilled at keeping secrets, and though she'd promised honesty from here on out, only time would prove it. Daniel needed to keep his wits about him. Especially given the risk to Owen.

Nothing would happen to the little boy. Not on his watch.

Refocusing on the case, he continued, "The men who've attacked you haven't tried to kill you. Instead, they've attempted to kidnap Owen to gain your cooperation. Gideon wouldn't do that. He'd kill you to ensure the evidence is never found."

Ellie mulled that over and gave a slow nod. "That tracks. But how did Tobias even find me? And why does he think I have the evidence?"

Jonah gestured for the remote, and Daniel handed it over. With the skill of an experienced gamer, he navigated to a video on social media. A group of teenagers performed a choreographed dance in Silver Creek's town square. Jonah paused the video and pointed.

Ellie was frozen in the frame, exiting an ice cream shop with Owen on her hip.

"That's how Tobias found you."

She blinked incredulously. "From a social media post?"

"This one went viral," Jonah said. "Over fifty million views."

"Fifty million?" Ellie rose and began pacing the room like a caged tiger. "I've spent the last three years refusing to have my picture taken, and I get outed by dancing teenagers and a viral post. Unbelievable. Does Gideon know where I am?"

"We don't think so." Daniel had promised her honesty, and that's what she would get, even if it hurt him to scare her. "Not yet. The attacks are too uncoordinated. Tobias is smart enough to avoid jail, but his men aren't as careful as he is. Still, it's only a matter of time before Gideon figures out you're alive and that Tobias is using you to find the evidence Lena collected."

"I don't have the evidence." Ellie came to an abrupt stop, the carpet covering the wood floor bunching under her feet. "I never did. Otherwise, I would've handed it over to the FBI years ago."

"It's possible Lena gave it to you without your knowledge," Jonah offered. "Or she left a backup somewhere. A place only the two of you would know."

Ellie's forehead creased in concentration as she considered those options. "I suppose it's possible, but that wasn't her style. Lena didn't trust anyone. She only handed off files in person. Even then, she used encryption codes..." Her expression brightened with realization. "What if the FBI recovered something from the warehouse where Lena and I were shot? They may have the evidence but not realize it."

Cole leaned forward in his chair, planting both feet on the ground. "Wouldn't the FBI have gone over that scene with a fine-tooth comb and examined anything electronic they found?"

"Not necessarily," Jonah said. "Lena was dead. The warehouse was used by transients. If the evidence wasn't obviously connected to the case, or was encrypted beyond their ability to crack, they might've archived it with the rest of the digital overflow."

Ellie bobbed her head in agreement. "Lena was paranoid. She could've hidden the evidence on a burner phone or a generic flash drive. Something ordinary enough to be logged and forgotten if no one knew what it was, especially if it wasn't found on her body, but somewhere nearby."

Daniel had to admit it was possible. Evidence from chaotic scenes like that warehouse sometimes fell through the cracks, especially if resources were pulled to other cases.

"How does the FBI mole fit into all of this?" Ellie asked. "If Gideon doesn't know I'm alive, and Tobias is the one after me, then why didn't anyone respond when I called the emergency line?"

"We don't know." Daniel massaged his temples. A headache was brewing. "We can't even confirm there is a mole. It's possible the attackers tracked your personal phone, and that's how they found us at the hospital.

We're being cautious by not informing the Bureau until we know more."

The front door opened. Lieutenant Rodriguez strode in, her expression dark. She'd been outside coordinating with local and county authorities to track the suspects. From the look on her face, the search hadn't gone well.

"The perpetrators may have acted like reckless fools," Vikki announced, "but they planned their escape well enough to evade capture. I suspect this stunt was designed to frighten Ellie into finding the evidence."

Daniel quickly brought her up to speed on their discussion. Vikki considered Ellie's theory for a long moment. "How would we find out what evidence the FBI collected from the warehouse without alerting the Bureau?"

"My former boss, James Callahan, would know," Ellie offered. "He's retired now, but he was responsible for processing the warehouse. He knows I'm alive but doesn't know my new identity. The Bureau created it using internal systems and buried the paperwork under layers of red tape so deep only a few people could ever find it. James was the one who insisted on that. He wanted to make sure no one, not even the Bureau itself, could track me down. But if anyone could give us answers without putting me or Owen at risk, it's him."

"Jonah, track him down, please." She directed her attention back to Daniel. "In the meantime, I want your surveillance footage. Ryker and Gavin are pitching in to help on the case."

Ryker Montgomery and Gavin Sterling were

members of their ranger team. Both men were exceptional investigators, and Daniel was glad for their help.

"We'll try to identify the shooters and tie them to either Tobias or Gideon," Vikki continued. "We've also collected bullets and casings. If their weapons were used in another crime, it could help us identify them."

Daniel inclined his head. "Don't forget the blood from Mr. Broken Nose. Chief O'Neal sent it to the lab. We should have the DNA results by now."

Vikki pulled out her phone. "I'll follow up."

Progress. They still had more questions than answers, but there was forward momentum now.

Daniel prayed it would be enough. They needed to stop this for Ellie and Owen's sake. The men hunting her had made foolish mistakes, which gave them an edge, but all of that would change the moment Gideon or someone from the Iron Fist learned Special Agent Elizabeth Conway was alive and well.

Those men would shoot to kill.

TWELVE

Hours later, the gentle lull of the vehicle threatened to put Ellie to sleep. Country music played softly from the radio and miles of highway stretched beyond the beam of their headlights. Jonah hadn't been able to locate a phone number for her former boss, only an address. He lived about three hours from Silver Creek, in a tiny tourist town near the Brazos River.

Ellie prayed James would have answers.

She glanced at her watch. Another forty minutes to go. Night had fully fallen, and the darkness pressing in around them felt heavier now that they'd left the highway for a narrow country road. Daniel's gaze was fixed straight ahead, his profile lit faintly by the dashboard. He'd been quiet for most of the ride. The silence wasn't awkward exactly, but it had weight, as if he was mulling something over.

Ellie couldn't shake the feeling that he was having second thoughts about trusting her. She'd promised to be honest, but words were cheap. She'd have to prove herself through actions, and that would take time they might not have. The whole situation was frustrating. It was also her fault. Every step forward seemed to bring a new challenge.

What bothered her most—and she knew it wasn't logical—was how much his doubt stung. Somehow, Daniel's opinion mattered more than it should. And that only fueled her frustration. Her life was in chaos, and here she was trying to interpret mixed signals from a man she barely knew. She had more important things to focus on, for Owen's sake, if not her own.

Which reminded her... "Should we check on things back at the ranch?"

"We called twenty minutes ago." Daniel shot her a quick look. "I know it's nerve-racking to leave Owen behind, but I promise, he's safe. The ranch hands are on high alert, and Cole might joke around, but he takes his job seriously. He won't let anything happen to my mom or Owen."

He spoke with such confidence. It struck a chord. Ellie had once trusted her own team implicitly. But now, with a mole possibly buried in the Bureau, her ability to believe in anyone had eroded. "You trust him that much?"

"Absolutely." There was no hesitation. Daniel glanced at her again and a flicker of sympathy crossed his handsome features, but when he spoke, there was a hardness in his tone. "Not everyone can be bought, El. Cole is on medical leave because he was shot protecting his fiancée from a stalker. Instead of resting, he volunteered to help our colleague, Jackson Barker. Jackson was working on a murder case when the detective partnered with him was targeted by the killer. Her family was threatened. Cole protected them."

He focused back on the road. "I trust everyone in Company A, but Cole... he's proven himself over and over again. He'll protect my mom and Owen."

Guilt prickled her. "I'm sorry. I know not everyone can be bought, and I don't mean to disparage Cole. It's just... leaving Owen after everything that's happened is hard."

"That's understandable." He paused. "I'm sorry too. I should be more patient. You're protective of Owen and don't know Cole well. I forget how much I'm asking you to take on faith. And betrayal messes with your head."

She adjusted her seat belt. "Sounds like you're speaking from experience."

"Not professionally. Personally, yeah... I've been burned."

Ellie waited, but he didn't elaborate. That loaded silence settled between them again, causing fresh frustration. It wasn't logical to expect him to share personal details when he'd only asked for case-related honesty from her. But somehow his silence felt like proof that whatever trust they'd built was shaky at best.

To keep herself busy, she reached for the cell phone they'd purchased before leaving Silver Creek. The location settings were disabled, and she had a new phone number, so it would be difficult for anyone to trace. She opened a browser and searched for Gideon Voss.

A string of news articles and social media accounts popped up. The leader of the Iron Fist had cultivated a carefully crafted public persona—businessman, entrepreneur, political donor. Not much had changed in the last three years. She paused on a photograph of him with a state senator. Gideon was tall and good-looking, with blond hair and deep-set eyes. Dressed in a tux, with a glass of champagne in his hand, it would be hard for the average person to believe he was a drug dealer and human trafficker.

But she saw him for exactly who he was.

A criminal. A killer.

Daniel glanced at her screen and frowned. "I hate that he's still walking free. The rangers have worked hard to tie him to the Iron Fist, but there's never been enough direct evidence to bring charges."

"Gideon didn't get this far by being stupid. He's careful to keep his illegal activities at arm's length. His lieutenants do all the dirty work. He keeps them loyal by paying them handsomely and providing top-notch lawyers if they get into trouble."

Ellie opened a new tab and typed in Tobias Kincaid. Unlike Gideon, there wasn't much online about Tobias, but she found a mug shot from last year when he was arrested for the illegal possession of a short-barreled rifle. Tobias had none of Gideon's polish. His eyes were beady and mean, even in the grainy arrest picture. Tattoos covered his neck and traveled down his chest and both arms. His head was shaved bald, but he sported a beard that came to a harsh point underneath his chin.

"Did you interact with him?" Daniel asked, jutting his chin toward her phone. "While you were undercover."

"Yeah. Tobias was always the odd man out. Gideon is selective when it comes to his lieutenants. You have to work within the Iron Fist for years before entering the inner circle, but Tobias had an inside track. His brother, Eric, had been one of Gideon's most loyal lieutenants before he died in a drug bust. Gideon took Tobias under his wing after that. But Tobias lacked self-discipline. He never gained the respect of the other lieutenants, especially Adam Parish."

"That's Gideon's right-hand man, right?"

"Yeah. His top enforcer." Ellie shivered. "I suspect he's the one who killed Lena and shot me, although I have no evidence to prove it."

Daniel reached over, laying a hand gently on her arm. "We'll get them. All of them, if we can."

His words and the touch sparked a flight of butterflies. She looked out the passenger window, trying to ignore the attraction, watching as the town lights grew brighter.

Minutes later, Daniel slowed as they turned onto a quiet residential street. Porch lights glowed, casting halos in the night. Lawns were tidy, and American flags fluttered on several mailboxes. When they approached the address Jonah had found, Ellie blinked in surprise.

Cars were everywhere. Lining the curb, crowding the driveway, even parked across the street.

Daniel slowed further and pulled to the side. The house was well kept with a wide porch and maintained flower beds. Every light in the house was on. Laughter and music drifted faintly from the open windows. The smell of grilled meat hung in the air.

"Looks like we crashed a party," Daniel murmured.

Ellie craned forward. "James has a big family. Maybe it's a birthday or anniversary."

Daniel put the truck in Park but didn't shut off the engine. "Stay here."

Ellie gave a small nod, her nerves fluttering again as she watched him cross the yard and climb the steps.

A woman in her late 60s opened the door. Blonde hair. Red apron. She smiled at Daniel and stepped onto the porch. Then James appeared behind her. His gray hair was longer than Ellie remembered, and he'd grown a beard. He looked... comfortable. Casual in his jeans and a faded Texas Longhorns T-shirt. James stepped around the woman, said something to Daniel, and then his gaze shifted to the truck.

His expression changed instantly. His eyes narrowed, his mouth flattened into a grim line. He stared at Ellie through the windshield with none of the warm familiarity she was used to. Instead, he appeared downright hostile. She lifted her hand in a tentative wave.

James didn't wave back.

He shared a clipped exchange with Daniel, then

turned and disappeared into the house. A second later, the front door slammed shut.

Daniel returned to the truck at a measured pace, his jaw tight. He climbed in and shut the door.

Ellie angled toward him. "What did he say?"

"He'll meet us at a diner off the highway in half an hour," Daniel said, putting the vehicle into Drive. His gaze swept the neighborhood. "He said we shouldn't have come. I told him it was urgent, that we had no other choice. I get the impression James believes he's being watched."

"Watched?" Tension coiled through her body. "By who? The Iron Fist? Tobias? Or the FBI?"

"I don't know." Daniel pulled away from the curb, his attention on their surroundings. Searching for any sign of danger. "But we may have just made everything worse by coming here, El."

THIRTEEN

One mistake after another. Today had been full of them.

Letting his guard down around Ellie when he should stay professional. Check. Alluding to his failed marriage during the car ride. Check. Driving Ellie to see her old boss and potentially exposing her to more danger... double check.

Daniel sipped his ice water and wondered if he was making yet another mistake by following James's instructions.

The diner had seen better days. Battered checkered flooring, saggy booth seats, and rickety tables were stuffed between a worn-out kitchen and a sad-looking front desk. Several truckers were perched on the chrome barstools, but most of the tables were empty. A gas station occupied the other half of the building, and several rigs were parked around back. Large windows provided a view of the highway. The stink of fried onions and despair hung heavy in the air.

It'd been forty-five minutes. No James.

The bathroom door creaked open, and Ellie emerged before rejoining Daniel at their table. She'd positioned her chair right next to his, giving her a view of the diner's exits and entrances. The scent of her shampoo teased his nostrils. She smelled like wildflowers and honey, reminding him of summers on the ranch. A silent battle warred within him, the desire to lean closer fighting with the urge to put space between them. The smartest move would be to hightail it out of here. If Daniel didn't think he'd have to throw Ellie over his shoulder to do it, he would've already left.

Nothing about this felt right.

Ellie picked up her fork and prodded the sad slice of cherry cobbler on her plate. Her vanilla ice cream had melted into a pale puddle. She leaned closer to Daniel. "If I eat this, do you think I'll get food poisoning?"

He smothered a laugh. "Several of the truckers at the bar are scarfing it down, so I'm sure it's safe."

"They have stomachs of steel. A couple of them are drinking the coffee, and I'm pretty sure it's sludge." She eyed her own mug before daring to pick it up and sip. Ellie winced. "Tastes like mud."

"Don't be such a wuss. It can't be that bad." Daniel took the mug from her and drank. The liquid was gritty, and thick enough to chew. He nearly gagged. "Okay, never mind. You're right."

Her eyes sparkled with amusement. "Never bet against me, Perez. You'll lose every time."

Daniel was momentarily mesmerized by her teasing

smile. Then he forced himself to look away and scan the diner. A flicker of hurt flashed across Ellie's face, and guilt stabbed him before he shoved it away. He needed to stay sharp. Even simple banter with Ellie was distracting.

A tired-looking couple entered and took a booth near the window. Still no sign of James.

"I don't think your boss is coming." Daniel took a long sip of his water to wash away the bitter taste of the coffee.

Ellie's mouth flattened. "He'll show."

"How can you be so sure?"

"Because I trust him. Like you trust Cole."

A minute later, a sedan pulled into the lot. James stepped out, surveying the area before heading toward the diner. Despite the warm evening, he wore a windbreaker, probably to conceal a handgun, and a ball cap pulled low. The former FBI Special Agent in Charge was pushing seventy, but he carried himself like a lawman with even strides and a steely-eyed stare.

He greeted Daniel with a nod before offering Ellie a tight smile. "Sorry I'm late. Getting away from my son's birthday party wasn't easy, and I had to make sure I wasn't followed here."

Ellie leaned forward. "Who's watching you?"

"I'm not sure." James dropped his keys on the table and angled his chair toward the front entrance. His hand landed briefly on Ellie's arm, his expression softening with something close to fatherly affection. "I suppose your sudden appearance means something's gone wrong."

"Very wrong." Ellie gave him a quick rundown of

everything, starting with the attack in the church parking lot and ending with their theory about Tobias.

James listened without interrupting. His face was unreadable, but the lines around his mouth deepened when Ellie got to the part about her emergency call to the FBI. There wasn't a flicker of surprise in his expression.

Daniel clenched his jaw. Had James known about the mole and left Ellie to fend for herself? He wanted to ask, but training and instinct held him back. The last thing they needed was to alienate the one man with answers.

When Ellie finished, James lifted his cap and dragged a hand through his hair. His attention locked on Daniel. Measuring him up. It reminded Daniel of the first time he'd met Ellie, and the way she'd done the same. Clearly, James had mentored her. "Ranger Perez, you and I never had the pleasure of working together."

"No, sir. But your reputation at the Bureau precedes you."

A waitress approached, depositing a fresh ice water on the table for James. He ordered the coffee and cherry cobbler. Daniel had the sense he was gathering his thoughts. But why was he stalling? Something about the man seemed off, although he couldn't put his finger on what. James seemed... tense. Jumpy, even. It was subtle, barely an impression, but it lingered like the stink of the onions in the air.

"James," Ellie directed the conversation back to her. "Tobias is searching for the evidence Lena stole. I need to know what was collected from the warehouse where she was killed. It's possible whatever they're looking for is sitting in an evidence locker."

"It's not." His mouth puckered around the straw, and he took a long drink. His gaze roamed the restaurant and parking lot before returning to her. "I had every item collected from the warehouse analyzed. It took over a year, and I had to fight for the funding, but I wasn't going to miss the chance to take down the Iron Fist."

Daniel felt his anger fade. Maybe he was misreading James's nerves as malicious when it was just worry.

Ellie slumped in her seat. "I don't understand. Why does Tobias think I have anything?"

"Because about a month after you were declared dead, a letter arrived for you at the office." James pulled out his phone and tapped on the screen, bringing up an image. The handwriting was feminine and hurried.

Elizabeth,

I know you must've been angry when I didn't show at the warehouse, but the risk was too great. Gideon has grown suspicious, and I don't want to lead him to you. By now, you should've found the flash drive. It has everything you need to take him down. I made sure of it. Unlocking it won't be easy, but you're smart enough to find the answer.

I've made a lot of mistakes in my life. Too many. I pray this sets some of them right.

You were a true friend to me. One of the only two I've ever had. I'm sorry I left without saying goodbye. Trusting the FBI with my life wasn't a risk I was willing to take. It'll be better—and safer—on my own.

Stay safe,

Lena

Ellie's eyes filmed with unshed tears, but her voice didn't waver. "I don't understand. Lena was killed in the warehouse. How could she have sent this letter?"

"It was delivered by courier. Lena arranged it before she died. I went through everything in your office, but didn't find the flash drive she's referring to." James studied Ellie's expression. "I take it you don't know where it is?"

"No." Her brow furrowed. "Lena came to the warehouse... she was shot there."

"Gideon must've found out about your meeting somehow and stopped Lena before she could escape. He had her killed at the warehouse, along with you. Two birds. One stone."

Daniel held up his hand. "Hold on. If this letter arrived at the Bureau, then how did Tobias find out about it?"

James leveled a look in his direction. "Probably for the same reason no one answered Ellie's emergency call."

"There's a mole."

He gave a sharp nod. "Tobias isn't the only one who knows the evidence exists. Gideon does too. Three days after this letter arrived at our office, the Iron Fist upped the price on Elizabeth's head. And then yesterday, I got word from an old informant of mine that it'd been raised again. Three million dollars."

Dear heaven above. Daniel spoke through clenched teeth. "They know she's alive."

"They suspect at the very least." His expression was grim. "Gideon keeps track of Tobias. I'm sure he knows Tobias is searching for—or has found—Elizabeth." James's attention shifted to Ellie. Her complexion had gone pale and her muscles were stiff, but she was listening and thinking. He leaned forward. "You need to figure out where the evidence is. Whatever is on that flash drive can take down the entire organization."

Movement in the parking lot caught Daniel's attention. A dark-colored SUV drove into the lot. He tensed.

Ellie's voice cut through the air. "Why didn't you contact me when you discovered the letter?"

James's lips pressed together, a flicker of regret in his eyes. "Because your new identity was buried so deep I couldn't reach you. After the letter arrived, I tried everything I could to find you, but I hit a brick wall every time. The Bureau had sealed off your file and deleted any trace of your name change from the databases. With a mole in the FBI, I didn't dare keep digging, since I wasn't sure who could be trusted. I was afraid I'd expose you to whoever was leaking information to the Iron Fist."

Daniel kept his eyes on the SUV. "Do you know who the mole is?"

"I have my suspicions, but no evidence."

The SUV's passenger side window began to lower.

Daniel's heart rate spiked. "Get down!"

He grabbed Ellie and shoved her to the floor just as a hail of bullets shattered the front windows of the diner.

FOURTEEN

The sounds of shattering glass and screams filled the air.

Ellie's heart thundered against her rib cage as adrenaline and fear heightened her senses. The floor was cool against her heated skin. Bullets thudded into the wall above her, perilously close. Daniel's breath fluttered against her hair. His body covered her in a cocoon of safety, his arms cradling her against his broad chest. The world shrank as her vision narrowed to the assault rifle firing from the passenger side of a black SUV. She couldn't see who was holding it.

The bullets stopped as suddenly as they began. Tires squealed as the SUV took off around the side of the building.

Daniel shifted away from her. Gun in hand, he stayed low. Screams and cries from the other patrons echoed around them. Ellie sat up, her stomach swirling with nausea and her limbs shaky. Her vision dimmed at the edges. She sucked in a steadying breath.

A hand gripped her shoulder. Slightly rough. Urgent. "Where are you hit?"

Ellie quickly assessed her body, but there was no pain. She tried to push Daniel's hand away. "I'm fine. You—"

"You've been shot." Daniel's voice was tinged with panic. "El, you're bleeding."

Confused, she looked down. Blood stained her shirt. Her jeans. It pooled around her on the floor, dark and glistening beneath the flickering fluorescent lights. People were still screaming. Their terror fueled her own anxiety as she patted frantically at her side, neck, and chest. No pain. No gunshot.

An awful realization hit her as she looked at Daniel properly. Blood spattered his face and neck. Peppered his white shirt. Her heart stuttered as her hands stretched toward him. "It's not my blood, Daniel." Dread surged. "Is it you? Are you hit?"

A groan broke the moment.

James was slumped against the wall, blood soaking his chest and streaming down his left arm. His chair had toppled, trapping one leg beneath. Melted ice cream, cobbler, and crimson mixed on the floor around him.

Ellie scrambled to his side, shoving the chair aside. "James!"

His eyes fluttered open. "Didn't know... being shot... hurt this much."

Her composure wavered, but training took over. She yanked an apron from the kitchen rack and pressed it hard against the gunshot wound near his shoulder. James cried out. "I'm sorry. I know it hurts." Ellie didn't lessen the pressure. If she didn't slow the bleeding, he'd die right there.

Behind her, Daniel called for backup, his voice steady and clipped. The hysteria around them had dulled to a low murmur. Ellie didn't know if anyone else was hurt. The wall behind James was riddled with bullet holes. Most were clustered where she had been sitting.

Their attackers had been shooting to kill.

"Hurts..." His eyelids drooped shut.

"James, stay awake." Ellie's tone was sharp and commanding. "Paramedics are on the way."

A ghost of a smile touched his lips. "Bossy."

"You got that right. Don't you dare die on me, old man. You have people who depend on you, grandkids to spoil."

Ellie's chest ached with emotion. James had spent his life dedicated to the Bureau. Nights, weekends, holidays. He'd sacrificed time with his family to keep their country safe. He deserved to enjoy his retirement. Tears blurred her vision. It wasn't fair. An hour ago, he was attending his son's birthday party and now he was bleeding out on a dirty diner floor.

All her fault. This was all her fault. She never should've come here.

James opened his eyes and focused on her. "Don't trust anyone... find the flash drive... stop them..."

She nodded sharply. "I will. I promise."

Daniel disappeared into the kitchen and then returned. "The SUV is still here, and another has arrived. Men are getting out." He quickly took charge, herding everyone still in the restaurant toward a hallway that led to the adjoining gas station where they would be able to escape.

Sirens wailed in the distance. The police. Paramedics. Shouting erupted from the kitchen. A waitress and several chefs burst through the swinging door. Daniel directed them to safety, ordering them to lock the door behind them.

"Go." James's voice was barely a whisper. "Go now. They're coming. They'll make sure you're dead this time."

She pushed harder on his wound. It was still bleeding far too much. "I'm not leaving you."

Daniel appeared by her side. "El."

The sirens wailed louder.

James rallied, drawing his handgun from its holster before placing it in Ellie's hand. Then he looked at Daniel. "Get her out of here... won't shoot anyone else... she's the target..."

More shouting erupted from the kitchen. Metal clanged. Something crashed. A man's voice barked a command, harsh and purposeful.

Daniel gripped Ellie's arm, his tone urgent. "We have to go. Now!"

He hauled her to her feet. She clutched James's handgun, the weight oddly reassuring. Her former boss had shut his eyes. Playing dead? Or had he passed out? Sirens blared. Closer now. Maybe half a block away. She sent up a prayer that it would be soon enough.

Daniel pushed her toward the parking lot. Ellie raced across the restaurant, glass crunching under her tennis shoes. She slid on some water by the broken window before jumping the frame onto the asphalt. Daniel's boots pounded right behind her as they bolted for his vehicle.

A shout came behind them. Ellie ducked as bullets pinged off the surrounding cars. Glass in a nearby Toyota shattered, spraying her arms with fragments. She didn't dare slow down. Instead, staying low and moving quickly, she reached Daniel's Explorer. Seconds later, she was inside. He'd already fired up the engine. With a squeal of tires, he shot out of the parking spot. Flashing emergency lights exited the highway, heading their way.

Ellie lifted her head just enough to glimpse the inside of the diner. Men, dressed in black with balaclavas covering their faces, caught sight of the incoming police cars and bolted for the kitchen. One SUV circled around the side of the building. A parking lot spotlight caught the driver's face.

Dark hair, angled face, hawklike nose.

Adam Parish. Gideon's top enforcer.

The Iron Fist had found her.

Ellie's stomach twisted. She was now at the center of a turf war. Gideon wanted her dead. Tobias wanted to use her. Both men would stop at nothing to get the evidence Lena had stolen—either to use it or to bury it.

Daniel punched the gas as he tore out of the parking lot and shot down the feeder road. "Are you hurt?"

"No." She answered automatically but then paused to take stock. No gunshot wounds. That would have to do for now. "You?"

"No."

Her relief was short-lived. Police cars flew into the parking lot as the SUV driven by Adam sped onto the feeder.

He was following them.

Ellie's breath caught in her throat. "Daniel, that SUV—"

"I see it. Put your seat belt on. And stay low." His jaw clenched as his hands tightened on the steering wheel.

The SUV's headlights swerved behind them, picking up speed. Gaining ground. Ellie snapped her seat belt in place and realized she was still holding James's handgun. She adjusted her hold on the weapon. It felt both foreign and familiar at the same time. A tie to her old life, to the person she used to be.

Confident. Self-assured. Fearless. That's who Special Agent Elizabeth Conway had been. Being shot, losing her identity, and constantly looking over her shoulder had worn away those traits. Facing her past was difficult, and she didn't want to return to her life as an FBI Agent, but she'd joined law enforcement for a reason. She'd wanted to make a difference. To protect people. To do what was right, even when it came at a cost.

That calling hadn't disappeared. She'd just buried it,

along with every other part of herself when she changed her name.

A calmness she hadn't felt in a long time washed over her as a sense of purpose brought her sharply into focus. Daniel had saved her life. And if need be, she was prepared to save his.

God, give me strength...

FIFTEEN

Thunder rumbled as Daniel navigated a rutted backcountry road. Tree branches scraped along the side of his vehicle, each screech tightening the tension in his spine. He gripped the steering wheel harder, peering into the inky blackness ahead. The moon was buried behind thick clouds, and without headlights, the edges of the road were nearly impossible to make out. He was relying mostly on memory and instinct.

Finally, the trees opened into a wide turnaround and a rusted gate. Daniel executed a tight three-point turn before killing the engine. "I think we lost them. But we'll have to walk from here."

Ellie sat up straighter. "Where is here?"

"My cousin's vacation home. It belongs to his wife, since it was passed down through her family... long story short, the last name on the deed isn't Perez. Someone searching for us couldn't easily connect this place to me."

Daniel exited the vehicle and lifted the back hatch.

He quickly located the backpack stored in a side pocket and began filling it with water bottles and protein bars from his emergency stash. As a ranger, it was important to be prepared for anything. His cousin's house likely had supplies, but it didn't hurt to err on the side of caution.

Ellie appeared next to him, her slender form nothing more than a darker shadow against the night. "We aren't going back to the ranch?"

"Not yet. I want to make sure my vehicle isn't being tracked." Daniel slammed the hatch closed. "That's why we have to walk. It's five miles, give or take, to my cousin's place. We'll get cleaned up, rest, and head out in the early-morning hours for the ranch."

"What about Owen?" Ellie grabbed his arm.

"I spoke to Lieutenant Rodriguez when we stopped to get gas. Owen is well protected. Jonah volunteered to spend the night on the ranch to help Cole stand guard. Chief O'Neal has officers watching the place too. Plus, there are my ranch hands and the security system." Daniel took her hand and squeezed it. "You're the one in danger, El. I know it's difficult, but right now, the best thing is to steer clear of the ranch. Adam Parish was driving that SUV trailing us, which means those men who attacked us were from the Iron Fist. Their mission is to kill you. I don't want Owen or anyone else getting caught in the crossfire."

She was quiet for a beat. Then she interlaced her fingers with his. "Lead the way, Ranger."

Daniel hauled the backpack over his shoulder and, still holding Ellie's hand, moved away from the fence toward a path hidden in the trees. Thunder rumbled again. Rain wasn't far off, and the humidity was thick and sticky. Once they were deep enough into the woods, Daniel clicked on his phone's flashlight. The path was overgrown, roots and underbrush everywhere. He didn't want a twisted ankle added to their growing list of problems.

Ellie inhaled deeply. "Smells nice out here. Like evergreens."

"It used to be a Christmas tree farm. I spent a summer working here after college and before joining law enforcement." Daniel still knew every inch of the place by heart. "My dad and I were butting heads at the time, so staying at home would've been difficult."

"You and your dad didn't get along?"

"He expected a lot from me. As the oldest, he wanted me to take over the ranch. I had no desire to. It drove a wedge between us." He didn't often speak about that time in his life and wasn't sure why he was now. Maybe it was being here again, on this land. Or maybe it was because he wanted Ellie to know him better. "I lost my way for a while. Rebelled. Drifted from my faith and put distance between myself and my family. Eventually, Dad and I made up, but I took a couple of hard knocks from life before finding my way back."

Ellie sighed. "It's hard when your parents have a picture of who they think you're supposed to be. Mine were disappointed when I told them I wanted to join the FBI. They wanted me to be a college professor with lectures, tenure, a safe, tidy life." She gave a small laugh, dry and quiet. "They would've approved of my career as a mystery writer. Maybe that's why I chose it when everything fell apart."

He paused on the path to lift a branch. "After everything you went through, it's not wrong to need time to find yourself again."

"Maybe not." Her voice was soft. "But I'm starting to think I've been playing it safe. Hiding in this quiet, controlled life I built—writing books, caring for Owen, keeping my head down—because it felt easier than facing the part of me that used to run toward danger instead of away from it." She hesitated, then admitted, "I thought I was healing. But maybe I was just retreating."

Her words settled in the air between them, quiet and raw.

Daniel swallowed hard. He knew that kind of retreat all too well. After the divorce. After the miscarriage. After everything he'd hoped for had slipped through his fingers.

He'd buried himself in the job. Taken every case. Worked every holiday. Built a life that looked solid on the outside, reliable and predictable, but underneath, he was keeping his distance. From people and risk. From anything that might break him again. Maybe that was what had drawn him to Ellie from the start. Not just her courage or her grit, but the way she tried to carry her pain alone. The way she still showed up. Fought back. Loved that little boy with everything she had.

She swatted at a mosquito. The faint glow from the flashlight illuminated the dried blood on her clothes and the handgun tucked in the waistband of her jeans. Daniel's chest tightened. The harrowing escape from the diner drove home just how fragile their situation was. Ellie nearly died tonight. One bullet and the world would've lost this amazing woman with a heart of gold and the tenacity of a warrior. It hurt to think about.

She caught his look as she passed and stilled. "What?"

"Just..." He shook his head slowly, not knowing how to put everything he was feeling into words. "Glad you're alive."

Her lips parted slightly. "Pretty sure I have you to thank for that."

Thunder rolled overhead, deeper this time. A drop of rain landed on his shoulder, but neither of them moved. The flashlight flickered, casting shifting shadows between them. Ellie's eyes, a deeper gray in the low light, searched his. This time, Daniel didn't try to rationalize his way out of it. He moved closer, cupping her face in his hands...

And kissed her.

Gentle. A light brush of his lips against hers. Once. Twice. Giving Ellie the chance to pull away if she wanted. Each touch sent his heart rate into overdrive. Her breath whispered over his mouth as her fingers curled into his shirt. Daniel took the silent invitation and deepened the kiss.

The world tilted and spun as a rush of emotion crashed over him. Desire and need tangled with something deeper... something far more powerful. His heart thundered against his rib cage. Everything narrowed to this moment and the gorgeous woman in his arms. The warmth of her lips, the silkiness of her skin, the quiet surrender in the way she leaned into him.

He didn't want it to end.

But the rain fell harder, cold and steady. Daniel pulled back. Ellie looked up at him, dazed and beautiful in the flashlight's glow, and reality came crashing down like the storm above.

What had he done? This wasn't the time. Wasn't the place. They were in the middle of a manhunt. Killers on their trail. Owen still in danger. He'd gotten caught up in the moment and let his emotions override his judgment. Again.

History was repeating itself. Daniel had learned the hard way he wasn't built for romantic relationships.

The cracks in his marriage had started early. Different priorities. Mismatched expectations. His long hours and terrible communication. Her restless discontent. They were more often out of sync than not, but Daniel believed if he just worked harder, loved better, *tried more*, they'd find their footing.

Then came the miscarriage.

And everything that was fragile between them shattered. Daniel lost himself in his work, hoping to outrun the grief that he wasn't allowed to feel because his wife had been relieved by the loss. Freed. The distance between them grew until eventually she found someone else.

And when she left, her final words cut deep: *"You were a disappointment from day one."*

He took a step backward. "We should keep moving. The storm's coming in fast."

Ellie didn't argue. Didn't speak. Just nodded once. But he didn't miss the flicker of hurt that crossed her face before she tucked it away behind a mask of indifference.

As he focused on the trail ahead, his lips still warmed from their passionate kiss, Daniel told himself putting distance between them was the right call. Ellie deserved better than what he could give her.

So why did it feel like the biggest mistake of his life?

SIXTEEN

The one-story house appeared like a mirage in the darkness. Rustic, made of stone and wood, it was tucked between towering pines, its silhouette barely visible through the falling rain. Ellie shivered. Her clothes were soaked, droplets falling from her wet hair down the back of her neck. Her muscles ached from the five-mile trek, and every nerve was raw from the night's events.

She wasn't sure what hurt more—her legs, her heart, or the silence.

Daniel hadn't said more than a handful of words since pulling away from her on the trail. Not a single mention of the kiss. No apology. No explanation for his behavior. Just distance. The constant push-pull was wreaking havoc on her already fraught emotions. Once again, Ellie was struck by the notion that she'd be wise to keep her distance. And yet... she couldn't quite convince herself to actually do it. Not after the look she'd seen in Daniel's eyes before he stepped away from the kiss.

Like he cared for her more than he meant to. And it made him sad.

Daniel unearthed a hidden front door key from under a planter around the side. Warmth greeted Ellie as she stepped over the threshold, the musty air scented with cedar and something faintly sweet, like old pipe smoke. The open floor plan was cozy, with a stone fireplace, worn furniture, and thick curtains that blocked any view from outside. Rather than turn on the overhead light, Daniel flipped on a floor lamp. Thunder rumbled, vibrating the windows.

Ellie crossed her arms, trying not to shiver, but the soaked fabric of her shirt clung to her skin and chilled her to the bone.

Daniel noticed. Without a word, he disappeared down a short hallway and returned with a towel and a stack of folded clothes. "Take these. The shower's through there." He nodded toward the hallway behind him. "There should be hot water. I'll figure out something for dinner in the meantime."

"Thanks." She accepted the towel and her fingers brushed his. The contact was brief, but her pulse quickened. Tension radiated from him. There had always been an underlying attraction between them, but the kiss seemed to have morphed it into something far more potent. Daniel wouldn't even meet her gaze.

Tears pricked the back of her eyes as she hurried to the bathroom. Ellie shut the door and leaned against it. Across from her, a full-length mirror reflected the toll of the night. Dried blood stained her shirt, mud coated the hem of her jeans, and her socks were nearly black from grime. Her hair hung in limp, tangled strands. A streak of cherry cobbler marred her collarbone. Her eyes were red-rimmed from the effort of holding herself together.

She wanted to go home. Wanted to hold Owen in her arms, rock him to sleep, and curl up in her own bed with the baby monitor beside her.

The thought of her son broke the dam. Tears spilled down her cheeks, hot and silent. She missed him with a fierceness that stole her breath. Was he scared? Did Marta remember he hated peas? Had she given him his favorite bath toy—the green turtle with the cracked shell—and filled the tub with bubbles? Read him a story before bed?

Sucking in a breath, Ellie forced her runaway emotions back under control. Now was not the time to fall apart. There was too much at stake.

She showered with quick efficiency. The sweatsuit Daniel had unearthed was too big for her slender frame, but it was warm and soft. She finger-combed her hair and hung up the towel before leaving the bathroom. The soothing scents of chicken and warm bread tickled her nose. Daniel was stirring something in a pot on the stove when she entered the kitchen. "Smells good."

He looked up and paused, his attention lingering on her face. Concern flickered in his eyes. Ellie suspected he knew she'd been crying. She hugged her arms around herself, uncomfortable with how easily he saw through her. "It's been a long day. I miss Owen. I've never spent a night away from him."

"I'm sorry." He flicked off the burner on the stove. "If it makes you feel any better, Mom sent me a text saying that Owen had a good day and is sleeping soundly."

That made her feel better. Still, she couldn't wait to hold her baby in her arms again. "Any news on James?"

"Yes. He's out of surgery, and the doctors think he'll make a full recovery."

"Praise Jesus." Ellie hadn't stopped praying for her boss since escaping the diner. She felt a weight lift off her chest.

Daniel ladled soup into two bowls. "It's chicken and vegetables from a can. Hope that's okay."

"More than okay. I could eat the napkins at this point."

His lips lifted in a smile. "Mind cutting the bread? I found a loaf in the freezer and stuck it in the microwave to defrost."

They moved around the kitchen in comfortable companionship, setting the placemats, cutting the bread, filling water glasses. It was homey and domestic, and by the time they sat down to eat, Ellie felt more centered. More at ease. So when it came time to bless the food, she extended her hands across the table. "Will you lead us in prayer?"

Daniel hesitated and then took her hands in his. The warmth of his touch was comforting, the quietness in the kitchen making the moment intimate. Ellie bowed her head.

"Lord, we come to You with grateful hearts. Thank You for protecting us today. We pray for James, that he may feel the touch of Your healing hands. Keep Owen safe. Give us the wisdom to find the missing evidence, and the ability to obtain justice for the innocent people who need our protection. Last, Lord, we ask that You bless this food, so it may nourish our bodies and give us strength for the mission in front of us. Amen."

Ellie, touched beyond words at the fact that he'd included James and Owen in his prayer, gently squeezed Daniel's hands. "Amen."

His gaze met hers briefly, his eyes shimmering with unspoken emotion. Once again, Ellie was struck by the notion that his feelings for her ran deeper than he would like. She wasn't sure how to broach the subject. And now probably wasn't a good time for an emotionally charged conversation. They were both hungry and tired.

She picked up her spoon. Steam curled from the bowl. Ellie took a small bite, mindful of the heat, and made a noise of satisfaction. "This came from a can?"

"Yep. I dressed it up a bit with some spices and a little lemon." He flashed a boyish grin. "My mom has taught me a thing or two over the years." Daniel pointed at the slices of bread with his spoon. "Can't take credit for that though. My cousin must've made it."

The herb bread was soft and contained just the right amount of rosemary. Ellie spread a thick layer of butter on top. "Bread is my weakness. I can turn down sweets ninety percent of the time, but give me a loaf of fresh bread, and I'll eat the whole thing in one sitting." She groaned with happiness after taking a bite. "Okay, I need to meet your cousin and shake his hand. This is delicious."

"Family reunion in September. He'll be there." Daniel winked. "I'll ask him to bring a loaf just for you."

She chuckled. "I'll be happy to have it, although I don't know if I should crash your family reunion."

"No one will mind. There's hundreds of us anyway."

Her eyes widened. "Hundreds?"

"My mom has five siblings and my dad had ten. Just my immediate family, with my brothers and sisters, their spouses, and kids is twenty-five people. Sunday lunches are a circus." He shook his head as he spooned another mouthful of soup. "And the youngest, Juan, isn't even married yet. He's graduating college next week and intends to take over the family ranch. His girlfriend already lives in Silver Creek. It's only a matter of time before they get hitched and start multiplying too."

"Multiplying... you make it sound bad."

"No." A flicker of something crossed his face, but then it disappeared. "It's nice, actually. I enjoy having so many nieces and nephews to spoil. And my siblings have been fortunate in their marriages. They're all very happy."

Ellie broke off another piece of bread. "What about you? You never wanted to get married?"

"I was married. It didn't end well."

The words were matter of fact, but Ellie didn't miss the way his fingers tightened around the spoon. She waited for him to elaborate. He didn't. Getting information from Daniel was like pulling teeth. At least now she had some understanding of his hot and cold behavior. He wasn't trying to hurt her. It was clear whatever had happened in the past was coloring his present. It was also obvious he didn't want to talk about it.

She reached across the table and rested a hand on his arm. "Something is happening between us, Daniel. I'm not sure what it is, but I know nothing can move forward until you share with me whatever it is you're worried about."

He breathed out. "You're right, but I don't think I have it in me to talk about it tonight." He lifted his gaze to meet hers. "You deserve an explanation, and I promise to give you one. Soon."

It would have to do for now. Ellie gave a small nod and returned to her dinner. She smothered another piece of the homemade bread in butter. Her mind turned to everything they'd learned from James, including the message in Lena's letter. "I spent most of the car ride up here thinking about where the evidence could be. I'm at a loss."

Daniel took a sip of water. "Flash drives can be tiny. Lena could've hidden it someplace where it would be easily overlooked."

A long-buried memory bubbled to the surface and Ellie gasped. Her spoon clattered to the bowl and soup splattered on the placemat. "Two weeks before she died, Lena gave me a bracelet for my birthday. The flash drive could be hidden within it." Her mind whirled. "I was wearing the bracelet when I was shot."

"Where is it now?"

"At my house. In Silver Creek." It was one of the few things she'd taken with her from her old life into her new one.

Daniel's mouth flattened. "If the Iron Fist knows who you are, they're probably watching your place. Tobias might be too."

"I know. But the bracelet's well hidden. We'll be quick. In and out. Chief O'Neal can send someone to meet us."

"One cop won't stop them, El. They shot up a diner tonight."

He had a point. Her stomach twisted. "Anyone entering the house will be at risk. The Iron Fist won't hesitate to hurt someone to gain information on my whereabouts. Neither would Tobias. I can't ask someone else to take that risk. I have to go."

"You aren't going alone." His tone brooked no argument.

She opened her mouth to respond, but he raised a hand to cut her off. "No, El. We're a team. Where you go, I go." His expression hardened. "Now let's make a plan."

SEVENTEEN

By early morning, the thunderstorm had abated, but clouds hung heavy in the sky, promising more rain. Daniel's senses were on high alert as he turned into Ellie's neighborhood. The engine in his cousin's sedan rattled, vibrating the steering wheel. The old Toyota wasn't in the best of shape, but he hadn't wanted to use his official state vehicle in case there were eyes on Ellie's house. No need to announce their presence.

The residential street was quiet, not unusual for a Saturday morning. He passed two white-haired women in tracksuits and a man walking his dog along the retention pond at the back of the neighborhood before turning onto Ellie's street. Her house sat at the center of a cul-de-sac. Tactically, a nightmare. Only one way in and one way out.

Ellie adjusted the ball cap covering her sunshine locks. She was still dressed in the borrowed sweatsuit, the oversized shirt drooping off her shoulder to reveal creamy skin. Distracting. Daniel forced his eyes away, instead noting the way the hem of her pants draped over her ankle holster. At his cousin's place, he'd found a rig that fit James's Glock. The weapon was secure and, more importantly, concealed.

She craned her neck to look out the windshield. "I don't see anyone from the tactical team. Are you sure they're in position?"

Daniel's mouth quirked. "Notice the old man weeding his flowerbed two doors down? That's Jonah."

She squinted at the figure dressed in overalls and a white brimmed hat and then laughed. "Is he wearing Mr. Henry's clothes?"

"Probably." Daniel passed Ellie's house and completed the circle in the cul-de-sac before heading back the way they came. "More of my team are stationed throughout the neighborhood. We've got guys in the houses on either side of yours, and a drone giving us aerial views."

"You've got the bases covered."

He prayed that was true. With two gangs of killers on their tail, Daniel didn't know if any amount of backup would be enough. His gaze scanned the street, but there was no sign of trouble. If the Iron Fist and Tobias were watching the house, they were well-hidden.

Daniel turned down the next street and parked at the curb. They'd gone over the plan, but it didn't hurt to review it again. "We'll approach your house from the back, using the path along the retention pond. If you notice something suspicious, or recognize a member of either gang, then squeeze my hand twice."

He removed a set of earpieces from the cup holder and handed one to Ellie before putting the other in his own ear. The earbuds automatically connected to his cell. A faint buzz hummed over the line, a signal that the channel was live but the team was holding radio silence.

"We can hear the guys, but they can't hear us unless I activate the channel on my phone. In a pinch," he added, lifting a hand to his earpiece, "tapping once will open your mic."

"Got it." She shot him a charming smile. "Don't look so worried, Perez. I'm used to working undercover."

Daniel huffed out a breath that was half laugh, half frustration. He was being overprotective and bossy. "Sorry. I keep forgetting you're former FBI."

He scanned the street once more before exiting the vehicle and walking around to the passenger side. He opened Ellie's door and offered his hand. The moment her palm met his, Daniel's breath hitched. When she rose and brushed her lips against his, it sent a jolt straight through him.

Amusement made her eyes dance. "We're supposed to be a couple out for a stroll, remember?"

His heart kicked. "Right," he murmured. "Just try not to short-circuit my brain while we're at it."

That earned him a small chuckle. "I'm armed, honey. I'll protect you."

Despite the seriousness of the situation, he laughed, and giving in to his desire, pulled her close for another kiss. Nothing long. Nothing overt. Featherlight and brief, but it was enough to leave him aching for more. And when Daniel pulled away, he was secretly pleased to see that Ellie's eyes had darkened with desire and her amusement had faded.

She turned toward the path. "You're right. No more kissing."

"Uh-huh." Daniel caught up to her, slipping his hand back into hers.

The sidewalk was wide and lined with young trees. They greeted a woman walking a puffball of a dog. The cloud cover kept the temperatures pleasant as Daniel maintained a stream of conversation about his younger brother getting stuck in a tree when they were kids. His gaze never stopped roaming as he constantly watched for potential trouble.

His instincts warred with his emotions with every step closer to Ellie's house. She could handle herself—he knew that—but the idea of anything happening to her made his stomach knot. Daniel had to force himself to keep moving forward when all he wanted to do was rush her back to the ranch and safety.

"This is me." Ellie paused at a chain-link fence. The house was perched thirty yards up a small incline. Slipping her fingers through the gate, she worked the numbers on a combination lock until it popped open.

Daniel glanced behind them on the trail. A prickle of unease crept up his spine. He could feel eyes on him. His team? Likely. Still, it made his muscles tense. "I'm surprised you didn't replace the fence with a wooden one for more privacy."

"I thought about it, but I'd rather see the danger coming."

She shoved the gate open, and they entered the yard. A baby swing drifted in the light breeze, and water toys gathered around a small plastic pool with a slide. Overgrown bushes shaded the windows. Ellie's shoulders were tight as she pressed her finger to a pad on the back door and the locks snicked open.

Daniel checked over his shoulder once again. No one was there, but the feeling of being watched lingered. He pressed the Talk button on his cell phone. "Entering the house."

"10-4." Ranger Jackson Barker's response was immediate. He was the lead for this operation. "We've got your back."

The steady confidence in Jackson's voice was reassuring. It was only a few weeks ago that Jackson's life was put in danger during another case. Thankfully, both he—and his now-fiancée, Piper—came out of the ordeal in one piece. But if anyone could understand the nerves firing inside Daniel, it was his fellow ranger.

He dreaded the teasing that would accompany any meeting after this mission. Chances were, a member of the team had seen Daniel and Ellie kissing at the car. A mistake he shouldn't have indulged in. The rangers in Company A had a tendency to fall in love with the women they protected, a pattern Daniel wasn't doing a good job of resisting. An honest conversation with Ellie about his shortcomings needed to happen, and soon, before things progressed any further.

Ellie pushed open the back door. Daniel entered the house behind her, carefully stepping over broken glass and scattered silverware. The place hadn't been cleaned up since the break-in a few days ago. Drawers gaped open. The kitchen pantry was a wreck, and cabinet doors hung from the hinges. It smelled musty, even with the air-conditioning on.

Her gaze swept the space and her jaw tightened. Daniel placed a hand on her shoulder. "We'll clean it up after this is all over. Between my pack of siblings and the sewing circle, this place will be good as new in a few hours."

She nodded sharply, but her eyes were hard. Angry. "Let's get this over with."

Ellie led the way through the living room and into the hallway. The rest of the house was as bad as the kitchen. Pictures torn off walls. Furniture destroyed. Even Owen's nursery hadn't been spared. His tiny crib was broken in two places, jagged wood exposed like snapped bones, and little clothes were scattered across the floor. Stuffed animals had been ripped open. The sight of it churned Daniel's stomach. As did the destruction in Ellie's bedroom. The violation of her space ignited something primal inside him.

She didn't deserve this. Any of it.

Ellie ignored the wreckage and crossed to the walk-in closet. Dropping to the floor, she shoved away ripped clothing and pried at the carpet's edge. "I hid the bracelet here and nailed it down."

"Let me." Daniel moved past her and yanked at the corner, ripping the carpet up with brute force. Beneath it, tucked in a shallow cutout in the padding, was a plastic sleeve holding a diamond ring, a charm bracelet, and several papers.

His earpiece cracked.

"We've got movement." Jackson's voice was sharp and clipped.

Daniel tensed. His gaze snapped to Ellie even as his hand flew to the holster on his belt. He drew his handgun. Within seconds, she had done the same. He pressed the Talk button on his cell. "Status."

Static.

Gunshots.

They came from the front of the house. Shouts followed. Daniel heard his colleagues give the command for the shooters to put down their weapons, but then chaos erupted as a chorus of sounds made it hard to hear what was happening. An unfamiliar voice echoed in his ear. "FBI! Put down your weapons!"

Ellie's complexion was pale, her eyes round, but her jaw was set. She held her weapon in a steady two-handed grip.

Another round of gunfire. This time closer. The sharp crack of bullets splintering wood echoed through the house.

Adrenaline surged through his veins as Daniel's training kicked in. "Move. Now."

Ellie snatched the clear sleeve from its hiding place, and together, they darted out of the closet just as a fresh barrage of gunfire shattered windows in the living room. Heaven help them, were they surrounded? What was going on? Daniel tapped his earpiece. "Jackson, advise!"

Silence. Not even the buzzing letting him know the line was open.

The comms were down.

More shouting. A crash. The front door splintered as something heavy slammed against it repeatedly, each impact shaking the walls.

Daniel seized Ellie's hand and raced across the bedroom. He threw open the window leading to the backyard and stuck his head outside. Clear. For the moment.

He waved Ellie forward. "You first."

She pitched herself over the ledge and into the mulch below. Heavy footsteps thundered down the hall. As Daniel placed a hand on the windowsill, the bedroom door slammed against the wall.

Three masked men burst in.

Daniel threw himself through the window just as a bullet shattered the glass beside his head. Sharp fragments rained down on him as he hit the ground hard, the impact jarring his teeth. Ellie brought up her weapon and fired two precise rounds. Covering him. He caught a flash of her gorgeous face, focused and determined, every inch the FBI agent she used to be.

"Go!" he shouted, staggering to his feet.

They sprinted across the backyard. Gunfire tore

through the air. A bullet clipped the fence inches from Ellie's shoulder. She bolted through the open gate, Daniel one step behind her. His blood roared in his ears and he dared a look over his shoulder. The masked men were in the yard.

More gunfire.

A burning pain ripped through his leg.

He stumbled, his knees nearly buckling as his hand instinctively shot out to grab a tree branch. Ellie skidded to a stop and reversed course, reaching his side in a second. He could already feel the blood gushing, hot and fast, down his leg. He pushed her off. "Go!"

She ignored him, pivoting and unleashing multiple rounds at the men in the yard. They scattered like rats, seeking cover.

"Come on." She ducked under his arm and braced his weight. "Move, Daniel!"

He had no choice but to follow her instructions. He half-ran, was half-dragged, down the path along the retention pond, doing his level best to keep from leaning on her slender form too much. Blood stained the sidewalk. Every step was agony. It felt like the bullet was lodged inside him. Sweat beaded on his forehead, but he gritted his teeth and kept moving.

The gunmen would follow. And they'd kill Ellie.

Where was his team?

The path curved and his cousin's sedan came into view.

"A little further." Ellie's breath came in puffs. She, like Daniel, kept checking behind them for the gunmen.

Black spots danced in front of his vision. He blinked to clear them away, even as nausea swirled. It was fifteen more steps to the car, but it felt like five thousand. Daniel's knees threatened to buckle again.

"Go, El!" He tried to shove her away, but she refused to release him. She clung like a burr, her cheeks flushed with the effort of yanking him forward.

"No way, Daniel! Where you go, I go."

Even in his pain-induced haze, he heard his own words repeated back to him. And they hit like a sledge-hammer. They were a team. In another time, under different circumstances, it would've stirred quiet admiration—this woman who didn't flinch, didn't run, who fought beside him when it would've been easier to let go. Now, all he could process was the terror that she'd die trying to save him. It fueled his steps, pushing him beyond the bounds of what he thought was physically possible. Ellie was not dying today. Not on his watch.

They stumbled off the curb just as a white utility van screeched around the corner and came to a stop, blocking their path. Without thinking, Daniel shoved Ellie behind him and raised his gun as the sliding rear door flew open. A dark-haired man held up a silver badge. "Agent Tanner, FBI. Get in the van!"

Dizziness threatened to take him under as indecision froze him in place.

Then the unmistakable sound of shouting and boots pounded on the path behind them. A quick glance over his shoulder confirmed his fears. The gunmen rounded the corner.

Ellie pitched forward, wrapping an arm around his waist, and together, they dove for the van. Daniel hit the steel floor with a jolt, Ellie's soft form landing on top of him. Pain exploded in his leg. He barely had the chance to yank his feet inside before Agent Tanner slammed the door shut. Gunshots erupted like firecrackers, bullets pinging off the van's reinforced sides as tires squealed and the van lurched forward.

Hand shaking, Daniel sat up and aimed his weapon at Agent Tanner. His vision had narrowed to a pinpoint, and he was about to throw up from the pain, but he didn't trust either of the men in this van. Not with Ellie's life. "Who are you?"

"FBI, Ranger Perez. Put down your weapon."

Ellie's hand came up and grasped Daniel's wrist. She forced him to lower his gun. "He's telling the truth."

His gaze swung toward her. He swallowed. "You know him."

She nodded and said something he didn't hear as the blackness finally won and he passed out.

The clinic waiting room was as silent as a grave. Ellie paced back and forth, her footsteps muffled by the faded carpet. It had been over an hour since Daniel was taken back. He'd only passed out briefly, and they'd slowed the bleeding before arriving, but gunshot wounds could be unpredictable.

Agent Mike Tanner appeared in her path. He extended a takeaway cup of coffee. "Here. It's from the break room. Caramel. Your favorite."

"Thanks." Ellie accepted the cup and took a sip, eyeing her old colleague over the rim. His dark hair was thinner than she remembered, and lines feathered the corners of his eyes, but he retained his sensitive nature. Mike had always been one of the kindest members of her team. At one time, they'd been friends.

Now he was her jailer. But that wasn't entirely his fault. Mike was just following orders.

His gaze lingered on her face. A myriad of thoughts

played out across his features, but then he smiled softly. "It's good to see you, Elizabeth."

Camaraderie and warmth washed over her, along with a healthy dose of guilt. Until recently, Mike believed she was dead. She couldn't imagine what that must've been like for everyone on her team, hadn't let herself think about it. Betrayal took on many layers, and although she hadn't intended to hurt them, she had. "It's good to see you too, Mike."

He settled into a hard plastic chair. "So... you're a mom now."

"Sort of. I have a foster son, and I'm going through the adoption process." She took the seat across from him. "What about you? Still dating Patricia? I figure you two must be married by now."

He winced. "No. We broke up a few years ago. She couldn't handle the long hours and constant secrets."

"I'm sorry."

Mike shrugged. "Better to find out before we're married than after." His expression brightened. "My baby brother got into MIT, if you can believe it. He's a sophomore now."

Pride filled his voice, and it brought a smile to Ellie's face. Mike had practically raised his little brother after their mom died when he was eighteen. He'd put himself through college, joined the FBI, and somehow figured out how to balance career and parenthood. It hadn't been easy, but Mike had built a village around him—neighbors, teachers, church members, colleagues, and extended family. He was the reason Ellie had felt confident raising

Owen as a single mom, knowing she had her own circle of support.

"That's wonderful, Mike, but not surprising. Jack ran circles around our team in mathematics when he was in junior high. Remember how he used to challenge us to take the Mensa tests with him so he could practice? He'd cream us every time."

Mike chuckled. "Some of the guys refused to compete with him." His expression grew warm again. "But not you."

"I like a challenge." She sipped her coffee. "And it was a joy to watch him excel. Watching someone do something they're great at... it's inspiring."

The door leading to the exam rooms swung open and Special Agent in Charge Vincent Maddox strolled through. Maddox was the epitome of Bureau polish, from his pressed dark suit to his crisp white shirt and the blue silk tie knotted precisely at his throat. His blond hair was slicked back, and his ice-blue eyes swept the room with an assessing gaze. He carried himself with a confidence that had always struck Ellie as bordering on arrogance.

They had never seen eye to eye.

She rose. "How's Daniel?"

"Fine. The bullet was almost a through and through. The doctor excised it, cleaned the wound, and stitched him up. He'll need IV antibiotics and rest, but he'll make a full recovery."

Ellie let out a shaky breath as relief flooded through her. "Can I see him?"

"Not yet." Vincent's attention flickered to Mike.

"Tanner, keep Ranger Perez company while I speak to Agent Conway."

Mike nodded sharply and strode toward the exam room without casting a look in Ellie's direction. It was as if they hadn't shared that warm moment earlier. Vincent's presence had a way of wiping out anything that wasn't duty-bound and official. It bothered her that he'd taken over the team after James retired.

"This way." Vincent turned on his heel and started walking, fully expecting Ellie to fall in line behind him. She bristled, but there were questions she needed answers to. So she tossed her coffee in the trash and trailed him to a small conference room.

Vincent placed the protective sleeve containing the items from her house in the center of the table. He didn't sit. Neither did she.

"I'm going to ask you some questions, Agent Conway, and I expect answers."

Agent Conway. After three years in hiding, the title felt both familiar and foreign, like an old coat she'd long since outgrown. Ellie's mouth lifted in a sardonic smile. "I'm a civilian now, Maddox. And you haven't read me my rights."

He rested his hands on the back of a chair, his expression impassive. "Would you prefer I put you in a holding cell? Fingerprint you? How do you think your adoption application will fare when the judge learns you lied about your identity to the court?" He paused, letting the words hang heavy. "Right now, Agent Tanner and I are the only ones at the Bureau who know you're alive. That could change, depending on your coop-eration."

Her gut twisted, but she refused to let him see her fear. "What do you want to know?"

"Where is the evidence Lena gave you?"

She chuckled. "You think I have it?" Ellie shook her head. "You're a bit late to the party, Maddox. No one knows where the evidence is. That's why the Iron Fist and Tobias are hunting me down. Both of them would love to get their hands on it. And they're not the only ones." She watched his reaction carefully. "There's a rat in your department."

Not a flicker of surprise crossed his face. "What makes you think that?"

"No one answered the emergency number I called, for starters. I was left high and dry."

"Probably because no one except Callahan knew you were alive." Vincent held her stare. "When I took over as Special Agent in Charge, no one informed me of your name change or that you'd been given a number to contact. You might want to ask yourself why that is."

She inhaled sharply. He was suggesting James was working with the Iron Fist? What a preposterous idea. "During the first assault, I broke an attacker's nose. He never showed up to any emergency room in the state." She crossed her arms over her chest. "Maybe because his FBI contact set him up in an off-the-books clinic like this one."

"Or he drove to Louisiana." Vincent brushed off her

suggestion like an annoying pest. "We don't have much time, Agent. Let's stick to what's important."

He pointed to the objects on the table, which were the sum total of all the possessions she was allowed to take from her old life to her new one. Her mother's engagement ring, Ellie's original birth certificate, and the bracelet Lena had given her. "With two separate gangs hunting you down, what was so important you risked going back to your house for it?"

Ellie's mouth flattened into a thin line. Trusting Vincent was a risk. For all she knew, he could be the mole. But her options were limited. With a sigh, she pulled out the bracelet Lena had given her. It was silver with a lock charm and a cross. Grief rose unexpectedly, constricting her throat. She swallowed it down. "Two weeks before she was shot, Lena gave me this for my birthday. I thought it might be important."

Vincent nodded. "Go on."

Ellie examined the charms and noted, for the first time, that the lock appeared to have a crease on the side. Using the edge of her fingernail, she popped the charm open.

A piece of paper fell out.

Vincent snatched it from the table before Ellie could grab it. He unrolled the tiny slip and squinted. "Bestfriends422315730." He glanced at her. "What does that mean?"

"I don't know." Disappointment burned, but she shoved it away and quickly committed the message to memory.

Oh Lena, what kind of treasure hunt have you sent me on?

"Do you know where the evidence is?" Vincent pressed.

"No."

He scrutinized her, eyes flat and assessing. Then he tucked the paper and the bracelet into his pocket before checking his watch. "Ranger Perez should be done with his IV antibiotics by now. Agent Tanner and I will drive you back to his ranch."

Vincent scribbled a number on the back of a business card and slipped it into the protective sleeve with her things. "If you find the evidence or figure out what this message from Lena means, call me at that number."

Ellie reached for the sleeve, but Vincent didn't release it. He locked eyes with her. "You and I have never gotten along, Agent Conway, but I need you to trust that we're on the same team. Call me. No one else. Understood?"

Anxiety churned in her belly, but she returned his stare and lied easily. "I will."

Vincent eyed her suspiciously, as if he wasn't sure whether to believe her, but he released his grip on the sleeve. As she followed him out of the room, it felt like a thousand-pound weight settled on her shoulders. He wasn't helping her out of kindness. He was using her to find the evidence.

But why? For his own purposes? He'd always been ambitious, and taking down the Iron Fist would be a prime feather in his cap. Or was he the mole? If she contacted him the moment she got her hands on the evidence, he could hand it over to the Iron Fist and report back to the FBI that this was a wild goose chase.

She couldn't trust him. The only person she could trust was Daniel.

And that was more true today than ever.

Vincent stepped aside to speak to a doctor, pointing toward a room on the left. Ellie quickened her steps, shoving all her confusion aside, and focused on getting to Daniel. She heard him from the hallway. His tone was demanding and authoritative. "I don't care if you think I need more antibiotics. Get this IV out of me before I rip it out myself and hunt through every room of this place for Ellie. I'm done being patient."

She pushed open the door. Daniel was standing in the center of the room, an IV line stretching behind him. His hair was wild, his expression thunderous as he glared at Mike and a nurse. His right pants leg had been sliced mid-thigh and a thick bandage stretched down to his knee. He looked battle-weary and furious, but he was whole. Alive. She couldn't stop the tears from pricking her eyes.

"Don't yell at the nurse." Ellie marched inside and straight up to Daniel. She caught a flash of relief on his face before she wrapped her arms around his waist and pressed her cheek against his chest in a hug. "You're being a bad patient."

His embrace was immediate. Daniel breathed in deep, his fingers tangling in her hair. "You okay?"

"I'm fine. I wasn't the one who got shot." She pulled

back and then directed him to the bed. "Sit down and listen to the nurse so we can get out of here. I want to see Owen."

Now more than ever, she wanted to hold her son in her arms. Protect him. With the FBI in the picture, things had grown more complicated. More unsettled.

More dangerous.

Daniel's injury was a physical reminder of all her worst fears.

If she didn't find the evidence soon, none of them might survive.

NINETEEN

Two days after the shooting, Daniel's leg was swollen and throbbing, but he kept the pain at bay with over-the-counter medication. He couldn't lose focus with so much on the line. His team had gathered at the ranch, sequestering themselves in his father's old office to discuss the case. Not that they were any closer to figuring out where Lena had hidden the evidence. But reviewing what they knew might uncover new leads.... At least, he hoped so.

"When the FBI swept in, they threw the entire operation into chaos." Jackson scowled, a two-day growth shadowing his jaw. Dark circles marred the skin under his eyes. He likely hadn't slept a wink since the attack at Ellie's house. "They arrested the gunmen and have refused to share any information with us. Maddox won't even confirm who the men were working for."

Jonah popped a peanut in his mouth and chewed thoughtfully. "How did we miss the FBI altogether? They came out of nowhere."

"After the initial break-in, once they learned that Iron Fist and Tobias were looking for me, they bugged my house," Ellie reasoned. She sat on the couch with Daniel, his injured leg propped up on her lap, her hands lightly stroking his socked foot with absentminded tenderness that felt as natural as breathing. "When Tanner and Maddox picked us up, they were in a surveillance van. Could've been five miles away with backup on standby. That's how they got to the house so fast. It would've been impossible for you to spot them ahead of time."

Lieutenant Rodriguez frowned. "You can bet we won't make that mistake again."

Cole scoffed. "Everywhere we step, there's a SNAFU. Ellie was ignored when she used the emergency line. Mr. Broken Nose hasn't shown up at any hospital. No one has found him or the guy with the busted kneecap. The blood we recovered from the church parking lot has gone 'missing'"—he used air quotes around that word—"from the lab. The FBI just happened to have your house under surveillance during our operation and, oh, they arrested the gunmen but refuse to share information with us about them."

He prowled the room like a caged tiger. "Stinks of a cover-up to me." He glowered. "And so far, the common denominator is Special Agent in Charge Vincent Maddox."

The lieutenant held up her hand. "Tread lightly, Cole. I don't want to accuse anyone of being a mole until we have hard evidence of their guilt." She sighed. "I've initiated an investigation into the lab screwup, but so far, we haven't uncovered when the blood went missing. The lab can't even confirm they received it. The entire day's record was wiped from the computer and the backup systems. It's created a mess that'll take weeks to sort out."

"We don't have weeks." Daniel felt it in his gut. Since the shooting, things had been quiet, but it felt like the eye of a hurricane. He was waiting... bracing... for the other half of the storm to hit. "Have we learned anything new about Lena?"

Jonah sat up in his chair and tapped his iPad. "Nothing significant. Born April 22, 1997. She grew up in Briarwood, Texas, which is a tiny town about four hours from here. Mom was a truck driver; dad left the family when Lena was a baby. No siblings. She was raised by her mother and grandmother. Won a capture-the-flag—that's a hacking competition—at sixteen and got some notoriety from that. Left home at eighteen to attend college on a scholarship. She caught the eye of Gideon Voss when she won a state cyber challenge later that same year. It's unclear when their romantic relationship started, but Lena dropped out of college in her sopho-more year."

"It started almost immediately." Ellie sighed. "Lena was brilliant, but growing up in a small town, she was also very sheltered. Then here comes this handsome, rich man who wined and dined her. Gideon was married, but he told her they were separated."

"A tale as old as time," Daniel muttered. "Poor girl."

Ellie nodded. "She was in deep before she discovered the truth about who Gideon was, and by then, he controlled her. Who she saw, who she talked to." Her expression darkened. "He opened bank accounts in her name, linked her to criminal activity. Used her hacking skills to shelter and launder his money. She was terrified of him, and didn't think she could break free and go to the police until I approached her."

The room fell silent. Lena's story weighed heavily on them all. She'd tried to do the right thing in the end and had paid the ultimate price. Daniel reached for Ellie's hand. "Do you have any thoughts on what the message enclosed in the bracelet means?"

"No. It could be the code to open the flash drive, but where the drive is, I don't know."

"It could also be a clue," Jonah offered.

"But... leading to where?" Ellie frowned. "The numbers don't make sense. It's not a phone number, not a zip code, it's not even a set of coordinates—"

A knock on the office door interrupted her. Marta entered, carrying little Owen on her hip. The baby wore an adorable firetruck outfit complete with matching socks. He grinned at the sight of Ellie, and Daniel quickly moved his leg off her lap so she could take him.

"Sorry to intrude, ladies and gentlemen." Marta passed Owen over with a smile. "But dinner is ready. Can you put crime on hold for thirty minutes? Other-wise, my arroz con pollo will disappear before you can get to it. I love my kids dearly, but they can eat like wolves."

"Don't have to tell me twice." Cole bolted for the door, colliding with Jonah, who was also racing to be first. They squabbled for priority until Jonah planted an elbow in Cole's gut and slipped through the doorway. Cole winced but followed a second later.

"Excuse my rangers, Mrs. Perez," Lieutenant Rodriguez said, rolling her eyes. "They clearly left their manners at home."

"Not all of them did." Jackson rose to his full height and extended a hand toward Daniel, his expression tight with a flicker of guilt that didn't go unnoticed.

"Stop feeling bad, Barker. It's not your fault."

Daniel accepted the assistance, letting Jackson take most of his weight as he got to his feet. His leg throbbed in protest, but he limped into the hallway, trailing behind his mother, the lieutenant, and Ellie as they chatted about how boys never grew up. The scent of chicken and spices made his stomach rumble painfully, but his heart melted when Ellie glanced over her shoulder and said, "Sit in the recliner. I'll fix you a plate."

"You've got a good one there." Jackson clapped Daniel on the shoulder. "Don't screw it up."

Before he could respond, Jackson disappeared after the food. Daniel headed to the living room, which was packed with his siblings and their families. A cartoon played on the television. Several of his nieces and nephews presented him with colorful drawings to help aid his recovery. And when Ellie arrived with his food, he shifted in the giant armchair so she could sit next to him.

He wanted her near. Was coming to the conclusion that he needed her near.

And he had no idea what to do about it.

Daniel still hadn't shared his past with her, the truth

about his failures, his divorce, and losing his child. The more time that passed, the harder it seemed to find the words. But it wasn't fair. The sweet place they'd found—the one with longing looks and physical closeness—couldn't last. The sooner Daniel ripped off the Band-aid, the better for everyone.

If only he could bring himself to do it.

The next few hours passed in a blur of laughter and stories from the week. Even his ranger buddies and the lieutenant joined in, sharing family tales and funny moments from the field. Eventually, the evening drew to a close as people began leaving.

Daniel waved goodbye to his sister from his perch in the recliner, then ran a hand over Owen's curly locks. The little boy clasped the coffee table tightly with one chubby hand. Drool dripped from one corner of his mouth as he grinned and bounced in place, tiny feet eager and wiggly.

"Dude, we gotta work on your saliva situation." Daniel wiped at Owen's mouth with a napkin.

Ellie laughed. She was sitting cross-legged on the floor, picking up toys strewn across the carpet. "He's teething. His poor nose has been a faucet, and his gums hurt too."

Owen took a careful step to the side, still gripping the table. His grin widened.

Daniel's brow lifted. "He's working hard on walking, isn't he?"

"He can stand on his own, but every time I think he's gonna take a step, he falls down."

"Huh." Daniel shifted in the armchair and gently coaxed Owen to let go of the coffee table. "Come on, little man. Let's see what you got." With careful hands, he steadied Owen and slowly pulled back. "El, call him over."

She set aside the toy and opened her arms, her expression glowing. "Come here, Owen. Come to Mama."

Owen shifted his weight from one foot to the other, tiny hands flapping for balance.

"That's it, buddy," Daniel murmured, his voice low and encouraging. "You can do it."

He wobbled, his little legs like jelly, and for a terrifying moment, it looked like he might flop onto the floor. Daniel lunged forward instinctively, catching his tiny arm and steadying him again. "Whoa, easy there. One step at a time, okay?"

He let go again, though his hands hovered just out of reach. "Try again."

Owen's round cheeks puffed out with a determined huff. He took a step. Then another. His eyes locked on Ellie's face. Her arms stretched out, voice sweet and full of love. "Come to Mama, Owen!"

One more wobbly step. And then he was there, collapsing against her with a squeal of triumph and a giggle that burst out of his chubby cheeks. Ellie wrapped him in a hug, tears shining in her eyes. "You did it!" She covered him in kisses, eliciting another round of giggles from Owen.

Daniel had never seen a more beautiful sight. His throat constricted sharply.

"Please tell me someone got that on video." Ellie looked up, her eyes shining brightly with excitement as Daniel's family clapped and cheered.

Marta stepped forward, holding her cell phone. "I got it. Don't worry." His mother's gaze slid Daniel's way, and for a moment, he had the impression that every emotion flooding his insides was written clearly on his face. He tightened his jaw and swallowed down the emotion threatening to drown him. "Great job, Owen. I knew you could do it."

Ellie beamed. "He's going to keep going now. He'll be unstoppable."

Daniel smiled. "Just like his mama."

Their eyes met, and Ellie's expression softened. She rose, with Owen in her arms, and brushed a kiss across Daniel's cheek. "Thank you."

The warmth of her lips against his skin, the simple gratitude... it all tangled in his chest. He didn't dare speak. Instead, he just nodded.

Owen fussed and rubbed his eyes. Ellie hugged him closer. "Today completely wore him out. I'd better get the bedtime routine started before he has a tantrum." She turned and hugged Marta. "Thank you for recording it. I'm gonna watch the clip a hundred times."

Ellie said goodbye to everyone and disappeared into the back bedroom with Owen. The house grew quieter as the last of the family left. Daniel stayed in the recliner, his foot propped up, staring out the window into the night. Outside, Jonah and Cole passed by, their silhouettes moving through the shadows as they did their perimeter rounds. A constant reminder of the danger Ellie was still in.

"You look troubled, papi." Marta set a mug of tea down on a coaster at his elbow. Her blouse was speckled with water spots from doing the dishes, but there was no sign of weariness in her expression. His mother lived to feed and care for her family. Having them close always brought her happiness.

She pushed aside the magazines on the coffee table and perched on the edge. "What's going on in that head of yours? I have a feeling it has something to do with our Ellie." She gave him a knowing smile. "You're falling in love with her, aren't you?"

"No." The word came fast, automatic and without thinking.

His mother didn't flinch. She just lifted an eyebrow. "Try again, papi."

He rubbed a hand over his face. "I'm not in love with her. I can't be. We barely know each other."

"Your father and I dated for two weeks before we got married and had forty-five beautiful years together. Time doesn't always count in matters of the heart."

Daniel let out a dry laugh. "Have you forgotten I was married once? That didn't turn out to be any kind of fairy tale. Not everyone is meant for a lifelong commitment, Mom."

"Ellie is not your ex-wife."

"I know that." Frustration edged his tone. "But I

haven't changed. I'm the same man I was all those years ago. My job still comes first, I struggle to communicate, and feelings…" He shook his head. "I'm terrible with feelings, always have been. If I made a list of my failings, it would be a mile long."

He blew out a breath. "I can't even bring myself to tell El about my divorce, let alone the miscarriage and all the things I did wrong. The conversation needs to happen. I need to explain myself, but every time I try…"

Daniel stared out into the night. He couldn't tell her. Couldn't expose the worst parts of himself and see the admiration in her eyes fade.

Marta was quiet for a long moment, her silence comforting. Finally, she spoke, her voice low and certain. "Your failings don't make you unworthy of love, Daniel. They make you human. Marriage isn't about pretending to be perfect. It's about seeing each other's flaws and loving anyway—working together to soften the rough edges through compromise and understanding." She laid her hand over his, warm and reassuring. "But both people have to want that. They have to fight for it, every day. Your ex-wife didn't want that. She didn't see what a good man you are. But Ellie… I think she does."

Daniel swallowed hard, her words hitting deeper than he expected. "I don't know if I'm ready to try again."

"You don't have to decide that tonight," Marta said softly. "Just… don't close your heart because of one person's blindness. Not everyone sees love the same way." She patted his hand. "And pray about it. Ask for God's guidance. He'll show you the way."

Daniel nodded. His mom kissed his forehead, like she had when he was a child, and then left him alone with his thoughts. They rattled and tumbled in his head, circling in a mix of confusion that gave him a headache. Finally, he sighed and closed his eyes.

God, I'm not sure what to do. I care about Ellie. Mom's right, I'm falling in love with her. But can I be the man she and Owen need? Or will I screw this up just like I did before?

Whatever answer Daniel was hoping for, it didn't come.

The front door opened, and Jonah entered. His expression was grim, and when he stepped to the side, James Callahan strode into the house. His arm was in a sling, his complexion pale, and his hair windblown. He met Daniel's gaze. "Sorry to intrude, but I need to speak to Elizabeth. It's urgent."

TWENTY

Bestfriends422315730.

Ellie stared at the message she'd written over and over again in her notebook. She'd broken the numbers into twos and threes, added them, divided them, even run them through a decoding program. All to no avail. She knew they meant something but couldn't figure out the message Lena had left for her. Maybe she was going about this all wrong.

Picking up her new cell phone, she flipped to a photograph of the letter Lena had sent to the FBI office. She read it again. Something niggled in the back of her brain, just out of reach, but no matter how much she tried to focus, it wouldn't surface.

A small cough drew her attention to the portable crib in the corner. Owen lay there, his little brow furrowed in his sleep. Ellie's stomach tightened as she set the notebook aside and crossed the room. She pressed her hand lightly to his forehead. He felt warm, but not dangerously so. Still, she couldn't help the automatic surge of worry.

She slipped into the bathroom and returned with the digital forehead thermometer. Kneeling beside the crib, she brushed the device across his temple. It beeped quietly, and she read the number—99.3. A low-grade temperature, but nothing out of the ordinary for a baby who was teething.

Ellie let out a breath. She was being overprotective, a side effect of caring for a child with a heart condition. Every slight cough or runny nose put her on edge. Owen managed so well, especially since his surgery, but an infection could cause complications.

A quiet tap on the doorframe drew her attention. Daniel stood just inside the bedroom, his broad shoulders nearly filling the entrance. He started to say something, but his eyes flicked to the thermometer in her hand. His frown was immediate. "Everything okay?" he whispered.

"Fine." Crossing the room, she set the thermometer on her nightstand and then gestured for Daniel to step into the hallway. She followed, pausing only to leave the bedroom door cracked. Owen was normally a good sleeper, but teething had made him restless. She wanted to be able to hear him if he stirred.

Daniel waited for her in the hallway, his concern obvious. "What's up?" she asked softly.

"James is here," Daniel said. "He needs to talk to you."

Surprise rippled through her. It had to be nearly 10 o'clock, far too late for a casual visit. She held up a finger to indicate Daniel should wait, then slipped back inside the bedroom to grab the baby monitor. Device in hand, she followed Daniel down the hall to the living room.

James was pacing in front of the full-length balcony doors, the moonlight outlining his rigid form. He turned at the sound of their footsteps. Ellie's eyes swept over him, taking in the sling on his arm, the dark circles beneath his eyes, and the tension in his shoulders. Despite her concern, it was a relief to see him alive and upright.

"James." She hugged him carefully, mindful of his injury. "I'm so glad you're okay."

His lips lifted in a tired smile, but it didn't reach his eyes. "Sorry to drop by so late, but I got word that you spoke with Maddox." His gaze shifted to Daniel. "Would you mind giving us a moment alone?"

"No, Daniel, stay." She turned back to her former boss. "Whatever we discuss, he'll find out about anyway when I tell him. Might as well let him hear it firsthand."

James's mouth tightened in disapproval, but Ellie ignored it. Daniel had more than proven he was trustworthy. She gestured to a chair. "Sit. Can I bring you some tea? Or coffee?"

"Nothing, thanks." James eased onto the couch, wincing slightly as he adjusted his sling. Then his attention locked on Ellie. "You can't trust Maddox. No matter what he says, he has ulterior motives."

Ellie felt Daniel stiffen, but she didn't look at him, afraid James would pick up on their silent communication. Vincent had warned her against trusting James.

Now James was telling her not to trust Vincent. She lowered herself into an armchair. "What makes you think Maddox is untrustworthy?"

James glowered. "Because he's the reason I had to retire. Maddox pushed me out to cover his own rear, because I'd grown suspicious that he was leaking information to the Iron Fist." His eyes turned flint hard. "Once, I was working an informant who had information that could have brought the Iron Fist's smuggling operations to their knees. Maddox was supposed to handle a minor detail. Surveillance support, nothing more. But within hours of him being looped in, our informant was found dead. No trace of the documents he'd been carrying. Unfortunately, I couldn't prove Maddox was the one who leaked the information."

Ellie's pulse quickened. "Is that why you didn't tell him about my name change before leaving the FBI?"

"Precisely. I didn't trust him to keep you safe."

"Did you try leaking specific information to flush Maddox out as the mole?" Daniel asked.

It was a tactic often used in law enforcement. Feed a suspected leak false intel and see if it reached the wrong hands.

James nodded grimly. "I did. More than once. Each time, it went nowhere. Maddox is careful. If he's the mole, he's smart enough to use intermediaries, but every instinct I have tells me he's dirty." His gaze skipped from Ellie to Daniel and back again. "You can't trust him."

Ellie's mind whirled. She already didn't trust Vincent, but hearing James say it made her decision feel grounded in logic rather than emotion. "He's using me to find the evidence." She quickly recounted the van rescue and the conversation she had with Vincent at the clinic. "The message in the bracelet looks to be a code, but I can't tell if it's a clue leading me to the evidence or the code I use to unlock the flash drive once I find it. Either way, Maddox insisted I call him the moment I figure out what it means."

James exhaled slowly. "He's a slippery one. If I were you, I'd stick with the rangers. Don't inform anyone in the FBI of your movements, in case Maddox gets wind of it."

The advice was solid, but a niggle of worry kept her from fully embracing it. Had James implicated Vincent because he was truly concerned the FBI agent was dirty? Or was he running interference, attempting to disparage someone Ellie might hand over the evidence to before James intercepted it?

She kept these questions to herself, instead choosing to nod in agreement. "Thank you for the warning."

James hefted himself from the couch. "I'd better get these old bones home. It's late." He pulled Ellie in for a hug and whispered in her ear, too low for Daniel to hear, "Be careful, darlin'. The Iron Fist has connections everywhere and powerful allies. Trusting the wrong person will get you killed."

He backed up and looked her in the eye. His message was crystal clear. As much as Ellie relied on Daniel, she would be wise to tread lightly with the ranger team. It seemed like they had her back... but so did Maddox.

Anxiety swirled in her stomach. Was James trying to help? Or was he trying to isolate her so she'd lean on him alone?

"If you need anything, I'm always here for you," James added, his expression earnest. "Day or night."

"Thank you." Her voice sounded hollow, even to her own ears. This entire case was making her question everyone, and she hated it.

James shook Daniel's hand. "Ranger Perez."

"Sir." Daniel limped his way to the front door and opened it for James.

Ellie waited until he was gone before collapsing onto the couch, burying her face in her hands as she rubbed her temples. "It's like being in a pit full of vipers. I don't know where to turn or who to trust. Everyone is warning me about someone else."

Daniel gingerly sat beside her, wrapping an arm around her shoulders. "You can trust me."

She leaned into him, the tension draining from her shoulders as she let his presence soothe her. The soft scent of his cologne and the solid weight of his arm around her chased away some of the worry that had been clawing at her. She drew in a deep breath and released it slowly. "Yes, but what happens when we find the evidence? How do we make sure it ends up in the right hands?"

"We'll cross that bridge when we get there."

It wasn't an answer, but for tonight, it was enough. Ellie sighed and nestled closer to him, resting her head against his chest. The house around them was quiet, so much so she could hear the beat of his heart under her ear. So strong. So solid. It awakened a longing inside her she hadn't wanted to admit until now. She wanted a relationship with this caring man, a partnership that managed the hard times and shared the joyous ones.

Her heart skipped a beat when Daniel threaded his fingers into her hair. She tilted her head up, her breath catching as he leaned down to kiss her. Warmth washed over her, a sweet ache that bloomed deep in her chest. The kiss was tender but laced with heat, a soft pull that left her wanting more.

Daniel pulled away slightly, his breathing uneven. "El..." He lightly kissed her again, before leaning back, revealing the worry buried in the depths of his gorgeous brown eyes. "We should talk. About us... about my past..."

A spike of fear shot through her. Ellie placed a finger over his mouth. "Don't. Please." She lowered her hand to his chest, feeling the quick beat of his heart. From their kiss? Or from his own fear? She didn't know. "I want to hear it, Daniel. I do. But not tonight. Please just... let's table any conversation about us until after this case is over."

Deep in her heart, she knew Daniel was going to end things between them. This sweetness they'd found was only temporary. Pretend. But Ellie didn't have the strength to face that at the moment. Not with everything else going on.

She wanted to hold on to Daniel—to this romance—just a bit longer.

He searched her face, his expression softening. "El—"

"Please." She was close to begging now. At any other time, it would have been embarrassing, but the overwhelming panic at what he might say kept her shame at bay.

He cupped her face, his thumb brushing along her cheek. The callused pad of his thumb was rough against her skin, but his touch was infinitely gentle. "Okay. We'll deal with us after this case is over."

"Thank you for understanding."

His lips lifted in a soft smile. "Well, you're kind of hard to say no to."

She managed a faint laugh, relieved that everything would stay the same for now. Daniel hesitated, and then he kissed her again, soft and sweet, lingering as if he wanted to memorize the moment. She could feel his reluctance when he finally pulled away. Ellie rested her head on his chest, soaking in the warmth and quiet strength of him. She would have stayed like that forever, but exhaustion was catching up to her. She yawned. "I should go to bed before I fall asleep right here on the couch with you."

"There wouldn't be any complaints from me." Daniel released her, though, and smiled as she rose and extended a hand to help him up. "Really, El? If I use you to lean on, we'll both fall."

"I'm stronger than I look. Didn't I half-carry you down the path after you were shot?"

"Don't remind me." He used the arm of the couch as

a lever to rise and then glowered at her. "You could've gotten yourself killed."

She poked him in the stomach. It was like jabbing her finger into concrete. "But I didn't. So don't be such a grump."

They continued to tease each other good-naturedly as they wandered down the hall, their voices hushed whispers to prevent waking up Marta and Owen. At her door, Ellie kissed Daniel one last time before saying goodnight. She slipped into her room. The lamp on the nightstand illuminated her rumpled covers and the notebook she'd been working in. Lena's message called like a siren, but the exhaustion was pressing down on her muddled brain. Better to leave it for tomorrow morning.

She started for the adjoining bathroom, casting an automatic glance toward the portable crib. Her steps faltered. Owen's brow was damp with sweat, his cheeks flushed pink. She hurried to his side, pressed a hand to his forehead, and her heart lurched. He was burning up.

She scooped him into her arms. He whimpered, his tiny body curling against her. She didn't even bother with the thermometer this time. She knew it was bad. And there wasn't a second to waste. With Owen's heart condition, an infection could kill him.

Ellie pushed back into the hallway, her voice urgent. "Daniel!"

He burst out of his bedroom, a toothbrush dangling from his mouth, his eyes wide with concern.

"Owen has a fever. We need to get him to the emergency room. Now."

TWENTY-ONE

Morning light streamed through the blinds on the hospital window, forming shadows across Owen's small form in the tiny crib. He slept peacefully, Ellie holding his hand. Her eyes had finally drifted shut. Long lashes rested against her cheeks, hollowed out by worry and stress.

Last night had been a harrowing ordeal filled with questions from the doctors, medical tests, and medications. Owen's mild respiratory infection had escalated into something more serious, which had the potential to create complications due to his heart condition, but the doctors were hopeful antibiotics would halt the progression.

Daniel removed a blanket from the closet in the corner of the room. Careful not to wake Ellie, he gently unfolded it before covering her slender form.

Her eyes cracked open. "Owen..."

"He's sleeping. You should too." Daniel bent and

kissed her forehead, the wound on his leg pulling painfully with the movement. "I'll keep watch."

They'd admitted Owen under a pseudonym at the hospital, and so far, it seemed to have worked. There was no sign of the Iron Fist or any of Tobias's men. But Daniel wouldn't let down his guard.

Ellie's eyes drifted shut again. Daniel drew back, his attention lingering on her and Owen. A heady wave of protectiveness and tenderness washed through him. He'd walk through fire for this woman and her little boy. If Daniel had any doubts about his feelings, this incident had dissolved them. There was no going back. No walking away. He feared failing Ellie and Owen, but somehow, the thought of losing them had become far more terrifying.

A faint knock on the door immediately commanded his attention. Daniel's hand automatically went to the holstered weapon at his hip. He quickly moved to the window and peeked through the blinds covering the glass window that separated their room from the nurses' station. The tension immediately eased from his stance. It was Jackson.

Daniel opened the door and slipped out into the hallway. "Ellie and Owen are sleeping."

Jackson lifted the tray of coffees in his hand. The other held a bakery box. "I brought breakfast. Kolaches and donuts. There's an assortment, since I wasn't sure what Ellie liked."

Daniel's stomach rumbled. They sorted out what they wanted, and then he set the rest of the pastries, along with Ellie's coffee, inside the room. He rejoined Jackson in the hall. The coffee was rich and dark, the caffeine working wonders on his sluggish brain. "Thanks for the breakfast."

"It's nothing." Jackson sipped his own coffee. "How's Owen?"

"The infection is under control. They're just monitoring him now to make sure he doesn't have any complications." Daniel scarfed down the kolache in three bites before wiping his mouth with a napkin. "What's happening with the case?"

"I have two things to share. First, a confidential informant reached out to Jonah with the news that Tobias is dead. Gideon's enforcer killed him two days ago. We haven't been able to independently verify the info, but it could explain why there haven't been any new attempts to kidnap Owen."

Daniel breathed out. "I know it's not Christian to wish for a man's death, but.... I'll be honest, I hope that's true."

"No one would blame you." Jackson leaned his shoulder against the wall and lowered his voice. "I quietly looked into James Callahan and Vincent Maddox. Callahan's record is spotless. Maddox has a clean record too, but there's something... odd. A personal bank account in Maddox's name had large sums going in and out over the last year. Nothing obviously illegal—the money could be explained in thousands of ways—but it's enough to raise questions about where it's coming from."

Daniel's brows knitted. "The account's only been in operation for the last year?"

"Yeah. Opened thirteen months ago." Jackson sipped his coffee. "If Maddox is the mole, then he's been working for the Iron Fist a lot longer than that. It's partially why I'm not sure this implicates him. Not to mention, an FBI agent of Maddox's caliber would be smart enough to have an off-shore account for any kickbacks he was paid."

Jackson had a point. Daniel rocked back on his heels and kept his voice pitched low. "Can you trace the money?"

"Working on it. Since Maddox is with the FBI, we have to tread carefully. I don't want him to catch wind of what we're doing. Jonah is tracking down people who Lena spoke with in the days before she was murdered, but most of them won't talk. They're either part of the Iron Fist or terrified of Gideon. We haven't made any progress on uncovering where she may have hidden the evidence."

"Lena left those messages for Ellie. She was smart enough to put the evidence someplace only Ellie could find it." Daniel downed the last of his coffee. "Now that Owen is out of the woods, maybe she and I can brainstorm together and come up with some new ideas on where to look."

Jackson nodded. "Keep us updated. And call if Owen gets discharged. Someone will escort y'all back to the ranch."

"Will do."

Hours later, as the sun hit high noon, Daniel

breathed a sigh of relief as his Explorer rumbled over the cattle guard at the entrance to his family ranch. Ellie, looking refreshed from her brief nap and a lot of coffee, was seated in the back next to Owen, who was playing with his stuffed dog, Scout. The antibiotics had worked wonders. Owen's temperature was back to normal, and from the constant babbling, he was back to his normal cheerful self. It was a relief to hear him so happy.

Behind them, Jonah drove his own state vehicle. Still no sign of the Iron Fist, but it was only a matter of time before they made their next move. Daniel had taken a circuitous route back to the ranch to ensure they weren't being followed.

"Mom texted to say she made pulled pork for lunch." Daniel glanced in the rearview mirror and caught Ellie's eye. "And peach cobbler."

She made a noise of satisfaction. "I'm gonna go into a food coma after I eat." Ellie's brow furrowed in the cutest way. "You must be exhausted too. Sugar and caffeine can only keep you going for so long. We should both take a nap. Then we can work on figuring out where Lena left the evidence."

"Good plan." Daniel's phone beeped with an incoming text from Cole. He scanned it. "Looks like lunch and our nap will have to wait. Chief O'Neal just arrived at the house with Owen's social worker. They want to speak to you."

"It's probably a surprise home check." Ellie groaned and lightly smacked her forehead. "I didn't tell Maggie that Owen was sick. She's gonna lecture me about that."

"Well, she shouldn't." Daniel could feel his blood starting to heat as he parked his Explorer in his usual spot. A Silver Creek patrol car sat next to a ten-year-old Honda with peeling red paint. He killed the engine. "The doctor said that your quick actions saved Owen from spending days in the hospital, hooked up to IV antibiotics. She should thank you for being such a conscientious mom. No one would take better care of this boy than you do."

Ellie's belt clicked open, and then her hand was on his shoulder. "Thank you, Daniel. For everything."

He turned and their gazes met. Warmth and admiration emanated from her gorgeous eyes. They were captivating... her eyes. When guarded, they were a hard and unyielding steel gray. But once those protections were down, the color shifted into a lighter blue, closer to a summer sky just before a storm broke. His breath hitched.

"There's nothing to thank me for, El. I'm glad I could be there for you." His attention shifted to little Owen in the car seat. "For both of you."

Movement on the front porch broke the sweet moment as Chief O'Neal emerged from the house. His hangdog expression was haunted, and he looked stricken at the sight of Ellie holding Owen close as she climbed the steps. Daniel immediately placed a hand on the small of Ellie's back. Her muscles were tense. She also sensed something wasn't right. Roy held out a hand, silently asking Daniel to stay put. The screen door slammed shut as Ellie entered the house.

"I need you to know that I tried to stop this."

Daniel's heart leaped into his throat. "Stop what?" He didn't bother waiting for a reply, but hurried into the house. Maggie Lyons, the social worker, stood in the living room dressed in sensible heels and a summer suit. Cole glowered, one hand resting reassuringly on Marta's shoulder as she sat in the armchair weeping. Jinx, sensing his owner's sadness, was leaning against her leg, his dark brown eyes filled with worry.

Ellie's expression was pale as she held Owen closer. "There's an explanation."

"Is there?" Maggie's mouth was flattened into a hard line. "Then I'd love to hear it, Miss Brooks. Or should I call you Miss Conway?" She tossed a printout on the coffee table. A copy of a Texas state driver's license for Elizabeth Conway. The photo was five years old, but there was no denying that it was Ellie. "Do you have an identical twin sister I know nothing about?"

Daniel stepped forward, his anger sparking hot and fast. "There's no need to be sarcastic, Mrs. Lyons. Ellie is right. There's a reasonable explanation for what's going on. What I'm more interested in knowing is how your office found out about her name change."

"An anonymous tip. When my supervisor brought it to my attention, I dismissed the allegation. Imagine how foolish I must've appeared when it turned out to be true." Maggie turned toward Ellie. "You lied about your name in legal documents and in your interaction with the court. Whatever explanation you have will have to be shared with the judge. Beginning immediately, your foster care license is revoked. Owen is coming with me."

"You can't do that," Daniel snapped, positioning himself between Maggie and Ellie. "This child is under protective custody."

Someone had sabotaged Ellie. No wonder things had been quiet. Gideon had been planning his next move, and he'd likely used his mole inside the FBI to do it. As for Tobias... well, maybe the news Jackson had heard was accurate, and Gideon had eliminated his rival.

Daniel sucked in a breath and tempered his voice. "Separating Ellie and Owen is a grave mistake."

Sympathy leaked into Maggie's expression. "I understand your concern, Ranger Perez. The department will take every measure to keep Owen safe from harm. His new foster home is in another county and he'll be placed there under a pseudonym. Additionally, the foster father is a military veteran. I have briefed them on the threats against Owen and they will take extra precautions."

"That won't—"

Maggie held up a hand to cut him off. "Ranger Perez, you are arguing with a brick wall here. I have my orders. The decision is final, and Owen is leaving with me. The department has filed an emergency protection order, which will be heard by the judge within the next 48 hours. You and Miss Brooks are welcome to attend the hearing and argue your case there." Her expression hardened. "Although I can't imagine what explanation would justify Miss Brooks lying about her identity."

Roy moved closer. "Daniel, don't make this harder than it needs to be."

"Don't make it harder..." His hands balled into fists as the urge to punch someone swelled. Daniel was never violent, but the desire to defend Ellie and Owen had erased all logic. He was a man protecting the woman and child he loved.

Loved. The realization punched him hard and stole his breath.

And when he turned to face Ellie, the sheer devastation on her face ripped straight through him. Her complexion was ashen, and her body trembled as she clutched Owen close. The little boy, sensing her distress, clung to her, burying his face in the hollow of her neck. Cole's quiet rage and Marta's sobbing only added to the weight of the moment.

Desperation took hold. "What if my mother acted as Owen's foster mother?"

"There are procedures to be licensed, starting with a background check. It takes weeks to be approved." Maggie sighed. "I'm sorry. There's nothing to be done." She extended her arms toward Owen. "Miss Brooks, please give him to me."

Owen cried louder. Ellie pressed a kiss to the little boy's temple, and her voice broke as she whispered comforting words. "Don't be scared. You're going to go with Miss Maggie on a little adventure. Mommy will see you soon."

Ellie's lips trembled as she struggled to maintain composure for Owen's sake. She looked back at Maggie, her eyes now swimming with unshed tears that made them appear almost luminous. "He went to the hospital last night for a respiratory infection. The antibiotics are in the diaper bag. He needs to take them three times a day, and the foster parents need to monitor him closely for a fever. If it returns, or he becomes lethargic, they need to take him back to the ER immediately."

"Thank you. I'll make sure they know." Maggie gestured for Owen.

"He can't sleep without Scout." She touched the stuffed dog wrapped in Owen's chubby arm. "His favorite blanket is in the diaper bag. He likes to read after bath time before bed. He hates peas but loves to eat oatmeal with bananas in the morning." Her whole body was shaking now, her voice growing more desperate with each word. "What else? Oh, he loves 'The Wheels on the Bus'—"

"Miss Brooks, now." Maggie gently but firmly lifted Owen from Ellie's arms.

The moment Owen left her embrace, it was as if someone had torn away a piece of Ellie's heart. Her arms remained outstretched, as if she couldn't quite believe he was no longer there. Owen's face crumpled, his small hands reaching desperately back toward Ellie. His cries became raw, primal wails that seemed to echo off the walls. The sound of his anguish was like a physical blow to everyone in the room.

Daniel's rage climbed even higher. "This is a mistake!" He whirled toward Chief O'Neal. "You know removing Owen from my ranch is a risk to his safety."

Roy grimaced. "I can't stop this, Daniel. She has the official paperwork and the jurisdiction. My hands are tied."

This couldn't be happening. "Mrs. Lyons, don't do this."

Maggie ignored him, hefting the diaper bag over her shoulder. "I'll be in touch." She nodded to Roy. "Chief O'Neal, let's go."

Ellie frantically wiped at her tears, but they were falling too fast now to catch. "Wait. He needs his favorite bath toy."

She raced out of the room and down the hallway. Maggie was already at the front door and didn't pause. She continued on, Owen's heartbroken wails trailing behind her like an echo of pure anguish. Daniel stood in the center of the living room, bereft, unable to stop what had been put into motion. Seconds later, car doors slammed and engines fired up.

Ellie burst from the hallway, a green turtle in her hand. Her wild eyes swept the living room before she spun around and raced for the porch. "Wait!"

Her panic cut through his numbness, and he followed her outside. The chief's vehicle, along with Maggie's, was already halfway down the driveway. Ellie stood frozen at the bottom of the porch steps, physically shaking as if she was caught in a blizzard and not the heat of the Texas sun. Her gaze was hollow and haunted. Daniel forgot his own grief, which was nothing compared to what she was going through.

He moved toward her. "El..."

His fingers brushed her shoulder, but she jerked away. Without a glance or a word, she took off, her blonde hair flying behind her as she raced across the yard, still holding Owen's bath toy in one hand. She was escaping with her pain. He watched as she bolted down the path to the creek and disappeared into the trees.

Leaving Daniel with nothing but the sound of his mother's tears, his own helplessness, and a deep-seated fear for Owen's safety.

TWENTY-TWO

The creek bubbled and swirled around the rocks. Ellie crouched on the bank, under the shelter of the oak trees, her breath coming in shaky gasps. The torrent of tears had left her eyes puffy and her nose congested. A headache pounded at her temples. Inside, she was hollow. Numb.

Her baby was gone. And it was all her fault.

Why, God? Why?

Her faith had seen her through dark times. During undercover work within the Iron Fist's circle, after being shot, in starting her new life in Silver Creek, and while nursing Owen back to health. Even during these threats on her life and last night in the hospital, Ellie had leaned on God, knowing that He would see her through. But now, she felt abandoned by her Heavenly Father. Cast into a darkness she wasn't sure she'd be able to surface from.

Her arms ached for Owen, and all she had was the

plastic turtle. His favorite bath toy. He would cry for it and be confused about why strangers were caring for him. And that sent a new wave of tears tumbling over her swollen cheeks. She'd failed him. Utterly and completely.

Ellie had known there was a risk in withholding her name from the court, and from Child Protective Services, but she'd been under orders. She'd followed those instructions to protect herself and Owen. Now that mistake had cost her dearly. She would try to argue her case with the judge, but Ellie wasn't a fool. Lying on official documents... misleading the court... she'd perjured herself under oath. She'd be lucky if the judge didn't arrest her right there in the courtroom, let alone grant her custody of Owen again.

A set of strong arms came around her and then she was shifted against Daniel's broad chest. He cradled her close, one hand cupping the back of her head as her tears soaked his shirt. He let her sob until she was spent again. Wrung out. The babble of the creek mixed with birdsong and the steady thump of his heart under her ear. Ellie wanted to push him away. She didn't deserve the comfort, didn't want it, but her body was spent after a long night in the hospital and the emotional turmoil of losing Owen. There was no strength left in her.

Daniel's mouth brushed against the top of her head. "You didn't fail him, El." His voice was rough with emotion. "You've been the best mother that little boy could ask for."

At another time, it might've struck her as strange that he was able to read her thoughts, but in this moment, all she could think about was how wrong he was. She started to shake her head, but his fingers threaded through her hair and gently massaged the back of her neck. "No, El. This isn't your fault." He grew quiet for a moment, a sigh escaping him. "I know what it feels like to lose a child. To blame yourself for something that was out of your control."

His words shocked her. Ellie drew back until she could look him in the face. And what she saw there was pain and grief. A mirror of her own feelings.

"My ex-wife and I... we lost a baby. Miscarriage at five months. It was one of the hardest things I've ever gone through. And I know it doesn't compare to your pain..." He wiped away a stray tear lingering on her chin. "Sweetheart, I'd walk over hot coals to take this away from you if I could, but I can't. What I can do is be down in the darkness with you, holding you up, letting you know that you aren't alone. It's what I wish someone had done for me."

"You..." Her voice was sandpaper rough from all her crying. "You went through that alone?"

"My family tried, but..." He shrugged. "My dad and I weren't on good terms at the time and things were strained. My ex-wife was relieved when we lost the baby. Our marriage had been on the rocks even before she got pregnant. In hindsight, I can see we were very different people, but I took my vows seriously and thought we could work things out. If we fought hard enough, if we loved each other enough... things would be okay."

He swallowed hard, his attention drifting away from

her to the creek. "Shortly after the miscarriage, she started having an affair with her tennis coach and left me."

Ellie inhaled sharply. Her own pain was momentarily forgotten as her heart bled for Daniel. "That's... I can't imagine how that must've felt."

"Awful. It felt awful." He let out a shaky breath. "We divorced over ten years ago, and I've avoided dating since, convinced that it was my mistakes that led to the breakdown of our marriage. I worked too much. I'm not good with my emotions and avoid difficult conversations. The grief over losing our baby... it compounded everything. She was so relieved that it happened, I couldn't share my sadness. We weren't in the same library, let alone reading the same book."

Loneliness bled into his voice. It hurt to think of Daniel blaming himself for the downfall of his marriage and grieving the loss of a child he'd so clearly wanted.

"I convinced myself that was it for me," he continued. "That I'd spend the rest of my life alone, and maybe that was for the best. Then you showed up with Owen and everything I thought I knew about myself... about what I was capable of feeling... it all changed. Still, I fought against it."

She'd known that. She placed a hand on his chest. "Why?"

"Because I'd failed once before, and I was certain that I'd never be the kind of man that you and Owen need. I'm flawed, El. Deeply flawed. I will probably always work more than I should. It takes a long time for me to sort out my emotions, and even when I do, it's difficult to find the words to explain them. I'm quiet. A homebody who prefers a walk next to the creek rather than a wild night on the town. And then there's the age gap. I'm nearly fifteen years older than you, sweetheart."

He gently smoothed a strand of hair off her forehead. "I could make a long list of all the reasons I'm wrong for you. Believe me, I've been over and over them a thousand times. But it hasn't made a lick of difference." His fingers trailed along her cheek, his gaze meeting hers once again. "I'm in love with you, El."

Her heart stuttered and her mouth opened, but no words could squeeze past the giant lump in her throat. Just when she thought she was all dried out, fresh tears swelled in her eyes. She drew in a shaky breath. "You can take your list and throw it into this creek, because I see you for exactly the man you are. Strong and capable, kind and loving. Someone who loves his family deeply and cares about his community. The kind of man who gets a phone call from his mother and drops everything to help a stranger because she asked him to."

Daniel inhaled and his hand trembled against her chin. She reached up to take it. "You walked straight into danger, protected Owen and me, because that's who you are. I see you, Daniel. The good and the bad, and believe me, the good far outweighs any of your faults." She stared into his brown eyes and knew without a doubt that every feeling she had for him was real. Ellie had wanted it to be pretend. Had been terrified to say the words out loud, or even admit them to herself, but she couldn't do that anymore. "I love you too."

Relief and wonder flooded his expression. Then Daniel framed her face with both hands and kissed her. His mouth was warm against hers, a balm to the hurricane of emotion inside her. Stillness followed. Ellie's world narrowed to the man holding her so tenderly, loving her so completely. This moment between them was different, this kiss unlike any they'd shared before. It was full of promise.

When they finally broke apart, Daniel rested his forehead against hers, both of them breathing hard. "Fight with me, El," he whispered, his voice raw. "I know you're hurting. I know this feels impossible. But I need you to fight with me."

She pressed her lips together to keep them from trembling. She wasn't alone in this, and whatever happened next, whatever trials she faced, Daniel would be at her side. It gave her strength and courage. Ellie leaned back to look him in the face and nodded. "I'll fight. For us. And for Owen. Whatever it takes, no matter how long it takes, I'll keep fighting."

Daniel's expression warmed, like the sun coming out from behind a storm cloud. He kissed her again, a quick brush of his lips against hers. "I love you."

"I love you too." Ellie wanted to linger in the moment, to relish in the momentary joy she'd found, but things wouldn't be right until she had Owen back in her arms. So she dusted the grass off her hands, picked up Owen's bath toy, and rose. Now that her head was clear and her emotions back under control, a fresh sense of urgency took hold. Owen had been moved to a new foster home, and although measures had been taken to keep him safe, she was well aware of the Iron Fist's reach. "We have to figure out what Lena's message means."

Daniel used the oak tree to pull himself to his full height. "Agreed." He grabbed her hand and held her in place. "But first, we pray. For Owen. And for us."

Ellie's jaw clenched tight. At the moment, she was too angry with God to speak to Him.

As if he'd read her mind again, Daniel squeezed her hand. "Don't shy away from prayer just because you're mad. God can handle it. Believe me, I've had a lot of angry conversations with Him. The important thing is to keep trying, keep reaching out. He hears you, El, even if it feels like sometimes He's not listening."

She hesitated and then nodded. Taking Daniel's other hand, she bowed her head. "God, we come to You with heavy hearts and painful anger..."

TWENTY-THREE

An hour later, Ellie speared a lettuce leaf with her fork and forced herself to eat it. Marta's food was amazing, but the pulled pork sat like a lump in her stomach. Eating was a necessity, not a pleasure. Her body needed fuel for whatever came next, and if she was going to get Owen back, she had to stay strong. Daniel had also been right about the prayer. She'd poured out her anger and hurt to God, and when it was done, nothing had changed except her. She felt clearer. More focused.

Determined to do anything and everything to stop the Iron Fist.

She chewed the lettuce and studied the long stretch of butcher paper Daniel had taped to the wall in his father's old office. He'd mapped out a timeline of the attacks, hung photographs of their suspects—Gideon Voss, his enforcer, Adam Parish, and their rival Tobias Kincaid—next to an aerial picture of Silver Creek. He had also printed a blown-up copy of Lena's letter and placed it next to the message hidden in the bracelet, Best-friends422315730.

Daniel stood with his arms crossed over his chest, a furrow creasing his brow. "Jonah ran the numbers in Lena's message through a decryption program but didn't come up with anything. We've been through them in a multitude of ways. Researched Lena's last days and come up empty. Maybe we're looking at this from the wrong angle."

"What do you mean?" Ellie set her fork down and wiped her mouth.

"We're trying to decipher Lena's message using the bracelet, but maybe what we should be focusing on is the timeline." He pivoted toward her. "Let's run through everything we know, but not in the order we discovered it—"

Her eyes widened as she immediately understood his train of thought. "But in the order *Lena* intended for it to be discovered." It was such a simple idea, Ellie felt foolish for not thinking of it herself. She pushed away from the table and grabbed a marker. "First, Lena gives me the bracelet for my birthday. Unbeknownst to me, there is a secret message hidden in the locket charm."

"Did Lena say anything specific when she gave you the gift?"

Ellie frowned, letting her mind wander back to that day. A pinch of grief threatened to take hold of her emotions, but she pushed it back. "She surprised me with it. In hindsight, I should've realized something was off, since we'd never given each other gifts before, but she said that we were friends, and friends celebrated each other's birthdays. Then she made me promise not to take the bracelet off. That I would wear it always." She tapped the marker against the table. "Lena was laying the groundwork even then to slip the evidence to me in secret."

Daniel nodded. "She had an escape plan."

"I can't blame her." Ellie returned to their new timeline. "Okay, Lena gives me the bracelet, then two weeks later she's murdered."

"Except she didn't plan on that. Lena intended to leave town. You would've been left high and dry without the evidence she'd promised you."

"True. Okay, let's assume this went as planned. One week after her supposed disappearance, a letter arrives by courier to my FBI office." Ellie tapped the letter. "This would've been the first contact I had with Lena after she fled town."

"The letter is the first clue."

Ellie pulled it down off the butcher paper and read it again. Daniel drew near, looking at the letter over her shoulder. The warmth of his body radiated against her back and made her pulse quicken. It was as if her body was attuned to his every breath now. She forced herself to focus on the letter.

Elizabeth,

I know you must've been angry when I didn't show at the warehouse, but the risk was too great. Gideon has grown suspicious, and I don't want to lead him to you. By now, you should've found the flash drive. It has everything you need to take him down. I made sure of it. Unlocking it won't be easy, but you're smart enough to find the answer.

I've made a lot of mistakes in my life. Too many. I pray this sets some of them right.

You were a true friend to me. One of the only two I've ever had. I'm sorry I left without saying goodbye. Trusting the FBI with my life wasn't a risk I was willing to take. It'll be better—and safer—on my own.

Stay safe,

Lena

Daniel tilted his head. "Lena says that between her disappearance and the letter's arrival at the FBI office, you should've found the flash drive."

Ellie tapped her nail on the table. "I know. That's why I assumed the message in the bracelet would lead to the next clue. But what if that's wrong? What if the reference to the flash drive was Lena's way of telling me that it existed?"

"Why not just say that?"

She considered his question. "Because she sent this to the FBI office. She couldn't ensure that I would be the only one to see it, and wanted it to sound like the evidence had already been passed along... like the job was done. If the mole read this, they'd think the flash drive was already in FBI hands, not still hidden somewhere waiting to be found."

Daniel's brows rose. "Smart."

"She was very smart. Okay, I get this letter and realize there's a flash drive of evidence." Ellie pointed to the end of the paragraph. "Here she mentions that unlocking the flash drive won't be easy… referencing the lock on the bracelet? It has to be. She intended for me to find the message hidden inside." Deflated, she spun around to look at the writing on the butcher paper. Best-friends422315730. "That brings us right back to square one."

"Not exactly. We know that Lena wrote this letter in code. The reference to the flash drive, along with the mention of unlocking and the reference to the bracelet proves that." Daniel rocked back on his heels, his expression distant, his mind working through the puzzle. "I believe your initial instinct was right. The message hidden in the bracelet is the code to unlock the flash drive. Which means that Lena intended for you to use the clues in this letter to *find* the flash drive."

Ellie couldn't argue with his logic. She went back to the letter and read it again, pausing when she hit the paragraph about friends. "You were a true friend to me. One of the only two I ever had…" A buried memory, one that had been niggling at her for days, suddenly surfaced. She inhaled sharply. "Lena once told me about a guy she dated in high school. Someone she loved deeply but left behind because she didn't want to stay stuck in their small town. She referred to him as a true friend."

Daniel was already moving toward his laptop. "What was his name?"

"Tyler Mitchell." It was a fairly common name and might produce hundreds of hits. Ellie hurried to his side. "Try narrowing the search to Briarwood, Texas. That's the town Lena grew up in."

Daniel's fingers flew over the keys, and then a moment later, he grinned triumphantly. "Got him! Tyler Mitchell, born July 30th, 1997. Lives in Briarwood, Texas. Drives a 2024 Chevy Silverado..." He clicked on the screen. "And it looks like he owns a bar called the Funky Monkey."

A few clicks later and a driver's license photo popped up on screen. Tyler was movie star handsome with a ruggedly outdoorsy look accented by his jet-black hair, beard, tanned face, and brilliant blue eyes. Ellie had no trouble understanding why Lena had fallen for him. A part of her wished her old friend had stayed in Briarwood and married Tyler, especially after she'd spoken so lovingly of him.

Ellie scanned the driver's license, noting the address. "Is the bar he owns also in Briarwood?" She glanced at her watch. It was after four. "If we start driving now, we'll probably have to catch him at work..." Her gaze fell on Tyler's birthday and her mouth dropped open. "No, it can't be that simple."

Daniel paused. "What?"

She snagged a marker and walked over to the butcher paper. "The message in the bracelet." She wrote out the message as she spoke. "Lena's birthday was April 22, mine is March 15, and Tyler's is July 30."

Best friends. 4/22. 3/15. 7/30.

Ellie capped the marker and whirled around to face Daniel with a broad smile. Her heart was racing with excitement, and she could feel the triumph lighting up her entire face. "Lena gave me the code to unlock the flash drive, but sent the actual evidence to Tyler. Then she buried the clues to both in the letter she sent to the FBI office."

Daniel rose, strode across the room in three quick steps, and swept her into his arms before planting a kiss on her lips. It was celebratory and exuberant. When he pulled back, his eyes were shining with pride. "I knew you'd figure it out."

"We, Daniel. *We* figured it out." She grinned at him, her hands still resting on his chest, where she could feel his heart hammering with the same excitement that filled her. The moment felt electric, not just from their breakthrough, but from the way he was looking at her. Like she was brilliant. Like she could conquer the world. It made warmth spread through her chest in a way that had nothing to do with solving the mystery and everything to do with being seen and appreciated by this incredible man.

But then a thought melted the smile from her face. "Do you think... was Lena murdered before she could get the flash drive to Tyler?"

His face clouded over with concern. "There's only one way to find out. Come on. We've got to get to Briarwood."

TWENTY-FOUR

The Funky Monkey was a low-slung, battered building that had seen better days decades ago. Neon beer signs flickered in the front window, fighting for space with hand-painted posters advertising live music and two-dollar shots. The parking lot was mostly dirt and gravel, pockmarked with potholes that glistened under the flickering glow of a rusted streetlamp. A handful of motorcycles and dented trucks were scattered across the lot.

Ellie's nose wrinkled. "First the diner, and now this dive. Why can't this case take us to the Four Seasons?"

Daniel's lips curved. "Are you a fan of expensive hotels?"

"I'm a fan of clean bathrooms and non-sticky floors."

Despite the tension coiling in his belly, he laughed and steered his mother's late-model Honda across the lot to a parking spot near the door. Marta's vehicle didn't have a GPS, which made it untraceable. They'd taken precaution after precaution before driving out to Briarwood. No cell phones. No electronics of any kind. With evidence mounting that there was a mole inside the FBI, Daniel wouldn't take any chances. His only method of communication with his team was an ancient flip phone his mother had kept in a kitchen drawer for emergencies —no GPS, no smart features, just basic calls.

He studied Ellie. She looked adorable in a black wig and glasses, selections taken from his mother's assortment of Halloween costumes. Her lips were painted a dark red, and she was wearing more eyeliner than he'd known was possible for any one person to wear. From the way she grimaced at her reflection in the mirror attached to the sun visor, Ellie wasn't a fan of her look. She rubbed her front teeth with a finger. "This lipstick is getting everywhere."

"You look beautiful."

She glanced at him and smiled. "You might need to have your eyes checked, Perez." Ellie waved a finger in front of her face. "Don't think this is a look you'll ever see again. I'm wearing enough makeup to be in a Vegas show."

"It's not the makeup. Or the wig." He brushed a finger along her jaw. "It's you."

She blushed, which only made the heavy rouge on her cheeks look even more dramatic. Ellie leaned closer and then stopped. "Can't kiss you. Lipstick."

"We're supposed to be boyfriend and girlfriend, remember?" He lightly brushed her lips with his.

She pulled back and then poked him in the chest. "No more of that. We're on business."

"Right." Daniel reluctantly released her and then exited the vehicle. His gaze swept the parking lot, an instinctive reaction more than out of necessity. A light drizzle had started, and it peppered his shoulders as he moved around the car to open Ellie's door.

She rose gracefully. Her blouse was deep red and long enough to cover the holster nestled at the small of her back. Ellie had traded James's Glock for one from Daniel's personal collection. Her jeans were worn and hugged her long legs down to her sensible boots. She'd have no trouble fitting in at a small-town bar. Daniel settled his cowboy hat on his head and led Ellie to the front door.

The interior was dim, thick with cigarette smoke and the smell of stale beer. Country music blasted from speakers overhead. Monday night was a slow evening, if the number of patrons was any sign. A few men were gathered around the bar, nursing drinks and watching the NBA playoffs on a large-screen television, while another small group played pool in the corner. One lone couple swayed on the scarred and worn dance floor.

"I don't see Tyler," Ellie murmured. "Maybe he's not working tonight?"

"I suppose, but it's his place. In my experience, most bar owners like to keep an eye on their establishments."

She nodded, and together, they crossed the room, peanut shells crunching under their boots as they went. Ellie slipped onto a stool at the bar and signaled the heavyset blonde tending drinks. The bartender's expression was friendly, her movements smooth and unhurried as she wiped down the bar with a white cloth.

"What can I get you, honey?" Her gaze traveled between Ellie and Daniel with a flicker of curiosity, but there was no tension in her stance. Just a steady watchfulness that said she'd seen it all.

"Two Cokes, please," Ellie said with a practiced smile. "Is Tyler in tonight? I'm an old friend of his, and I'd love to say hello."

The woman paused for a fraction of a second, then tipped her head slightly. "Oh, you're an old friend?" Her voice was light, as if she was in on the game, but didn't care to call it out. Probably thought Ellie was an ex. "Ty's in the back, working on the books. I'll let him know you're here." Her hand paused on the rag, blue eyes cool and curious. "What should I tell him your name is?"

Ellie's smile didn't waver, not for a heartbeat. "Elizabeth. He'll know who I am."

The woman's smile was small and understanding. She nodded once and moved down a hallway. Daniel sipped his soda, leaning against the bar casually to eye the patrons. Everyone seemed to know each other. Locals. No sign of any trouble. Still, his gut twisted uncomfortably. Especially when one of the men playing pool stared him down.

"Relax, Perez." Ellie's hand landed on his arm. Her voice was pitched low, although no one could likely hear her over the country music. "People like these can smell a cop from a mile away. You're giving off undercover vibes."

He shifted his weight to release the pressure on his injury. The swelling had gone down, but the thing still ached something fierce. "In case you hadn't noticed, we are undercover."

She chuckled. "Yes, but we're not interested in arresting the locals. You're making them nervous. Do I have to kiss you again?"

Daniel didn't have time to reply before the bartender returned. She tossed a thumb over her shoulder. "Y'all head on back. The office is at the end of the hall, past the bathrooms."

"Great." Ellie slipped away from the bar. "Thanks."

Together, they entered the dimly lit hallway. It was like something out of a horror movie. Soft padded walls. Bathroom to the left. An exit sign hanging crooked over a door to the right, and a broken neon light illuminating the sticky floor. Inexplicably, the scent of beer hung heavier back here than it had in the bar. Despite Ellie's admonishment to play it cool, Daniel could feel his anxiety ratcheting up. Ellie showed no sign of tension in either her walk or the easy knock she placed on the closed office door.

"Enter."

Ellie glanced at Daniel, and he gave a sharp nod to show he was ready. He sucked in a breath as she twisted the knob and the door swung open, revealing a shockingly neat office. An expensive laptop sat in the center of an oak desk covered in glass. Windows overlooked the back of the property, and a door on the opposite side probably served as a private entrance.

Tyler Mitchell stood near a whirling printer. He was dressed casually in a checkered button-down and dark jeans. A hefty belt buckle adorned his waist and rolled-up sleeves revealed a pattern of tattoos. Though his gaze flickered over Daniel briefly, it quickly settled on Ellie. The smile that followed was charming. Immediate. "Elizabeth, is it? I'm sorry, darlin', but I'm not sure I remember you. Have we met before?"

The hair rose on Daniel's arms. He couldn't explain it. Couldn't rationalize it, but something about Tyler felt off. A gut instinct honed from years of working law enforcement.

If Ellie noticed the same, it didn't show in her expression. She placed her hands on the back of a visitor's chair. "No, Tyler, we've never met. But we have a common friend." Her gaze locked with his. "Lena."

His brow furrowed in mock confusion as he pulled out his desk chair and sat down, setting the papers from the printer on his closed laptop. "Lena?" He puffed out a breath. "I haven't thought about her in ages. We were friends, but it was a long time ago." His charming smile never wavered. "How do you know Lena?"

Ellie raised a brow. "Let's cut to the chase, Tyler. You and Lena were high school sweethearts. I know that because she told me herself. I'm Elizabeth Conway, and I believe you know exactly who I am."

Faster than Daniel could blink, Tyler whipped out a gun from underneath his desk and pointed it at Ellie.

Instinct and training sent Daniel's hand moving

toward the gun holstered at his hip, but Tyler redirected his weapon toward Daniel.

"Don't do it, man. I've won shooting competitions thirteen years in a row. I'll put you on the ground before you can draw your weapon and have time to spare to shoot her too."

There was a thread of confidence in his tone, and Daniel instinctively knew it wasn't bravado. He froze. His heart thundered against his chest as the gun swung back to Ellie.

She raised her hands in the classic sign of surrender. "There's no need to shoot anyone. We aren't here to hurt you."

Tyler's expression was hard. "Agent Elizabeth Conway is dead. So I don't think I'll take your word on anything. In fact, I'd like to have one good reason I shouldn't just shoot you right now and save myself the risk of finding out just what you plan to do."

TWENTY-FIVE

The air thrummed with a powder keg of emotions. One wrong move and this would end badly.

For everyone.

Ellie kept her hands raised and resisted the natural human instinct to stare at the gun in Tyler's hand. Instead, she forced her gaze up. Undercover work sometimes required decisions to be made in a split second. This was one of them. She had little to go on beyond her own impressions. Behind the stony expression, there was genuine fear. Sweat beaded on Tyler's forehead and his focus darted between Ellie and Daniel.

He didn't want to shoot them. But Ellie would need to talk him down with logic. With the truth.

"The FBI faked my death because the Iron Fist put a price on my head." She kept her tone steady and soft-spoken, but her voice was filled with conviction. "It's true I was shot in the warehouse on the same day that Lena was killed, but I didn't die. I am Agent Elizabeth Conway."

Ellie kept her attention locked on Tyler, although she could feel the tension radiating from Daniel who was on her right. To his credit, he'd stepped back and let her take the lead. A difficult thing for many in law enforcement to do, but the goal was to get out of here alive.

"Last week, masked men attacked me in a church parking lot and attempted to kidnap my foster son," Ellie continued. "That's when I found out the evidence Lena had stolen was still out there somewhere. There are a lot of dangerous people looking for it, Tyler. I don't blame you for being cautious. But I'm not a threat to you." She gestured with her fingers toward Daniel. "Neither is he. Meet Texas Ranger Daniel Perez."

Tyler's brow lifted slightly, but he didn't lower his weapon. The suspicion didn't leave his face. "You could be lying."

"I'm not. I can prove it." Moving slowly, Ellie removed the glasses from her face and lifted off the wig. She deposited them both in the chair before raising her shirt to reveal the gunshot wound in her abdomen. The skin was mottled and white. "This is where I was shot. A few transients found me bleeding out in the warehouse and called 911, which saved my life. By the time I came out of surgery, the Iron Fist had put a price on my head. Going back to my normal life wasn't possible, so the FBI gave me a new identity. For the last three years, I've been living as Ellie Brooks in a small town close to here called Silver Creek."

She lowered her shirt. Her heart beat a rapid tempo as Tyler studied her face intently. Recognition dawned across his features, and he lowered his gun slightly, although he didn't relax his stance. Ellie nodded. "You know who I am."

"I've seen photos."

"Daniel has his Texas Ranger badge in the front pocket of his shirt. Can I reach for it to show you?"

Tyler gave a sharp nod. Ellie kept her movements slow as she turned. Daniel didn't take his eyes off Tyler, but as she removed his Ranger badge with her left hand, his fingers brushed against her right wrist. A light touch, one easily missed, but it had the weight of all the words he couldn't say.

Be careful. I love you.

Ellie's chest tightened momentarily. She drew in a steadying breath and placed the badge on the desk in front of Tyler. "Daniel is a Texas Ranger. He's been protecting me since the first attack."

"Why aren't you here with the FBI?"

"Long story short, there's a leak in the FBI. They can't be trusted."

"And you can?" Tyler countered.

She held his gaze. "Lena trusted me."

"And Lena ended up dead!" he shouted. Grief creased his features, but he locked it away and inhaled sharply. "How do I know you didn't kill her?"

"Because she was my friend," Ellie said softly. "She told me things, Tyler. About you. About the dog you rescued from the gas station and the silly way you used to put cheese puffs in her jacket pockets when she had a rough day. She said leaving you was the biggest mistake she ever made."

Tyler studied her for a long moment. His expression was unreadable, his breathing uneven. He was a man backed into a corner on the cusp of a decision. Ellie wasn't sure which way he would go. From the way Daniel shifted his body weight to the balls of his feet, readying himself to tackle Tyler if necessary, neither was he.

She held her breath, praying Tyler would make the right decision. "You and I are the only people Lena trusted completely. She sent the evidence to you, but she gave me the passcode to open it. Put the gun down. Let's work together to finish what she started."

He hesitated for one more second, then lowered his gun.

Ellie released a shaky sigh of relief. "Where is the evidence?"

He didn't move. "Did Lena really say that leaving me was the biggest mistake she ever made?"

Tears shimmered in his eyes, and they gut-punched Ellie hard, undoing the lock on her own grief. She felt her lip tremble as she fought back the emotion and nodded. "Yes. She loved you, Tyler. I'm sorry you both didn't get a second chance to set things right."

"So am I." He blew out a breath and holstered the weapon. "Sorry about holding y'all at gunpoint. Lena told me I could trust you, Agent Conway, but I've had a lot of strange things happen over the last three years and it's made me cautious."

"What things?" Daniel asked.

"My house and the bar were both broken into. Searched. It felt like people were watching me, off and on. Recently, there haven't been any incidents, but I've grown paranoid, especially since Lena's letter instructed me not to trust anyone, including the cops."

"The Iron Fist was looking for the evidence." Ellie glanced over her shoulder, and although the office door was closed, she could hear country music and the sound of laughter. A chill walked down her spine. Had the Iron Fist hired locals to monitor Tyler? Or was she becoming like him... paranoid and jumpy? She shot a worried look toward Daniel before focusing back on Tyler. "That's why they broke in. Why they've been watching you."

"That's what I figured." He marched over to a series of giant filing cabinets and pushed on the last one. It scraped against the concrete floor.

"Let me help you." Daniel joined him, and together, they shifted the heavy cabinet aside. Then they had to move the one next to it as well before a small safe hidden in the floor became visible.

Tyler bent down and rapidly typed in a code on the front panel. The safe popped open. He reached in and pulled out a single flash drive. "This is what Lena sent me."

Ellie's heart pounded against her rib cage. She rounded the corner of the desk and accepted the flash drive from Tyler. All this time... all the threats... there was a small piece of Ellie that hadn't truly believed she would ever find the evidence. Holding it in her hands was both a relief and a burden. They needed to get whatever was on this flash drive into the right hands ASAP.

Her gaze shot back to the desk. "Can I use your laptop?"

"Of course."

She was already moving to the chair and opening the computer. Tyler used his fingerprint to unlock the machine. Both he and Daniel stood on either side of the chair, watching over Ellie's shoulder as she plugged the flash drive in and quickly entered the password.

File after file appeared on the screen. She flipped through them in rapid succession, her heart beating fast with excitement at every new document. "Offshore bank accounts. Financial tracking of funds. Safe house locations where they store the weapons and drugs for sale." Her breath caught as a list of names popped up on screen. Ellie instantly recognized some of them from murders the FBI had investigated. "Sweet mercy, this is a hit list."

It was a treasure trove of information. Far more than she could have ever expected. No wonder Gideon was desperate to get his hands on it. His name appeared on many of the documents, including the financial ones. No amount of money or influence would keep him out of prison now. She looked up at Tyler. "Do you have another flash drive? I want to make a copy of this."

He fished one out of a drawer while Daniel used the flip phone to call his boss. Ellie half-listened as she attempted to copy the material to the second flash drive. It wouldn't work.

"I can't hear you, Lieutenant." Daniel pulled the phone away from his ear. He faced Ellie. "I don't have a signal in here. Be right back."

When he opened the door, a blast of country music and voices spilled out. Ellie barely noticed. She was too busy trying to copy the files over. Nothing she did worked. Frustration had her back teeth clenching. "Lena locked the files down somehow. We can't make a copy of them." She turned to Tyler. "Give me your phone. Hurry."

"What for?" Tyler asked, but handed it over anyway.

"I'm taking photos of the documents," Ellie explained, already snapping pictures. "I didn't bring my phone to prevent the Iron Fist from tracking us, but we can't risk having only one copy of this evidence." She also needed something smaller and more portable than the laptop, in case they were attacked on their way back to the ranch.

Tyler frowned. "You're keeping my phone?"

"Just temporarily—"

A crash from beyond the office door jerked her head away from the screen. Ellie half rose. "What was that?"

A second later, the bartender burst in. Her eyes were wide, and beer was spattered across her clothes. "Carl kicked off again." Another crash followed along with the sound of splintering wood. "We've got a bar fight."

Tyler cursed and ran around the desk. "Not again. They'll tear the place apart!"

The two darted down the hall toward the sound of flesh hitting flesh and glass shattering. Ellie debated following behind to help break up the fight, but she figured a bar fight in this neck of the woods was common enough that Tyler could handle matters. She went back to taking photos of the documents.

The phone lit up in her hand as a call came through. Unknown caller. Ellie ignored it, her sole focus on creating a second record of the evidence Lena had paid for with her life.

Then a text popped up.

Elizabeth, answer the phone.

She froze. Tyler's cell rang again. This time, she answered it.

"Hello, Elizabeth."

She immediately recognized the deep Southern drawl layered with mock amusement and more than a hint of cruelty. Adam Parish, the Iron Fist's top enforcer. A cold wash of panic gripped her insides, even as a mass of questions muddled her mind. How had he known to call her on Tyler's cell phone? To text her?

She scanned the ceiling, searching for a hidden camera. Stupid, stupid, stupid. Tyler mentioned his office had been broken into. To hedge their bets, it would've been smart for the Iron Fist to install surveillance devices.

"Yes. I can see you." He laughed. "You've been busy. So have I. There's a little boy with blonde curls and a stuffed dog named Scout right next to me. Here, Owen. Want to say hello to your mommy?"

Ellie's blood turned to ice as the familiar babble of Owen's sweet voice came over the line. She gripped the cell phone tight enough to make her hand ache as her body trembled with a mix of fear and fury. "If you hurt him—"

"Stop wasting time with empty threats. Remove the flash drive from the laptop and bring Tyler's phone with you. I'll text you the address once you're on the road. Oh, and leave the ranger behind. This matter is between the two of us." He paused. "It'll be good to see you again, Elizabeth. I've been waiting a long time to correct my mistake."

"You mean shooting me in the warehouse?" She scoffed, despite the terror running through her. "You had your chance at the diner, Adam. You missed. Two screwups in a row. Hard to be the top enforcer when you can't take out one FBI agent."

"Don't anger me, Elizabeth, or you'll regret it. Get moving. Tyler keeps the keys to his truck in the top left-hand drawer. No tricks, no secret messages. I have eyes on you, and your son is right here with me. If you want to protect Owen, you'll do exactly as I say." Adam hung up.

She was out of time. After ejecting the flash drive, she grabbed it, Tyler's cell, and the keys to his truck before racing to the door on the opposite side of the office. Humid night air washed over her when she opened it. Ellie stole one more glance over her shoulder, desperately hoping Daniel would be there, that he would see her leaving, but the hallway was empty.

She bolted into the night, her heart pounding with a single, searing prayer.

God, help me save Owen. Spare his life, even if you don't spare mine.

TWENTY-SIX

Each scrape of the windshield wipers grated on Ellie's ragged nerves. The coordinates Adam had texted to Tyler's phone led her down winding backcountry roads, each mile pulling her deeper into the wilderness. The last sign of civilization had been a rusted gas station thirty minutes ago. Clouds blocked the moonlight, and the steady drum of rain beat against the truck's roof like a racing pulse.

According to the GPS, she was less than two miles from the meeting place.

Her hands gripped the steering wheel. She'd been through her plan over and over during the drive. It was desperate, probably reckless, but it was the only card she had left to play.

The thick woods parted on the left, revealing a gravel road marked by a battered gate. Ellie's tires crunched over loose stones as she took the turn. Her stomach pitched and rolled with nerves, and her skin prickled with awareness as the massive iron bars swung open. She couldn't see them, but Ellie had no doubt there were men hiding among the thick trees and hidden cameras on the property.

She eased forward. The moment Tyler's truck rolled past the gate, the iron bars clanged shut again. Immediately, the air felt tighter in her chest. A side effect of being hemmed in with the enemy. Trapped. She forced herself to take a few deep breaths to counteract the adrenaline coursing through her veins and drive on. Owen needed her. She would not fail him.

The gravel road curved and twisted through the dense forest until, finally, it deposited Ellie in front of a massive house. Two stories tall, with jutting wings and manicured grounds, it looked like the estate of a wealthy recluse rather than the lair of a criminal enterprise. Did this house belong to Gideon? It didn't seem like his style. He was more flashy, more cosmopolitan. She doubted this place belonged to Adam either. He didn't strike her as the type who craved the trappings of luxury. Adam was a soldier. Brutal, focused, and unflinchingly loyal to the Iron Fist. He had no need for mansions or manicured lawns. No, this house belonged to someone else. Someone with power and money to burn.

She killed the engine, and like dark harbingers of death, three men emerged from the woods to surround her truck. All of them carried assault rifles with practiced ease, their eyes cold and dispassionate. None of their faces were familiar. Ellie swallowed hard. That they weren't wearing masks didn't bode well for her survival.

The driver's side door was yanked open, and rough hands dragged her from the cab. She stumbled, but they didn't give her a chance to find her footing. A brisk, impersonal pat-down followed. The handgun nestled in the holster at the small of her back was gone in an instant, as was the pocket knife tucked in her boot. Tyler's cell phone and the flash drive were also confiscated.

For a terrifying moment, Ellie feared the men would shoot her right there, but then she was grabbed by the arm and manhandled into the house. Her boots slid over marble in the foyer before sinking into thick carpet as her captors hauled her through a sitting room.

Enough was enough. Ellie suddenly shifted her weight, ripping her arms from their brutal hold. "I can walk." She drew in a breath, keeping her voice steady and noncombative. "I'm not going anywhere. There's no need to drag me."

One of the men, the leader of the group, grunted and then began strolling across the room. Ellie followed, the other two gunmen flanking her on either side. Thick drapes, expensive furniture, and unique artwork filled the space. Her ears were pricked for the sound of her baby's voice, but the house was as quiet as a tomb. The place was massive though. Owen could be anywhere.

Ellie lost count of how many rooms they went through before landing in a giant kitchen with a double island. The space was immaculately clean. Marble countertops and dark blue cabinetry played off of one another, punctuated by touches of greenery from the fresh herbs growing along the windowsill above the

Clutching Owen close to her chest, Ellie was forced to keep pace with Mike's frantic steps as he raced down a long corridor leading to God knew where. Hazy smoke hung in the air. If she slowed down an iota, the guard behind her jabbed her kidney with the barrel of his automatic weapon. She feared he'd accidentally shoot her.

Had he shot Daniel? Was her love dead?

The thought threatened to cripple her. Only the weight of Owen in her arms kept Ellie moving forward. She needed to find a way out of this for his sake.

Gunshots and screams echoed down the hallway. It was terrifying. The closest thing she could imagine to a war zone. Her heart thundered against her chest, and she struggled to remain calm. *God, lay Your loving hands over me. Owen is a helpless child who needs Your help. Please keep him safe. And please protect Daniel. I don't know...* She couldn't finish the thought. God knew the plea that was in her heart.

Mike stopped abruptly at a door and punched in a number on a keypad.

The guard panted. "We aren't going to the safe room, sir?"

"It's on the other end of the house," Mike snapped. "Feel like fighting your way through bullets to get there?" He yanked the door open and automatic fluorescent lights flickered on, revealing a garage containing several vehicles.

The guard jabbed Ellie in the back to spur her on. Mike led them past the sports cars, their footsteps echoing off the concrete. The room was chilly, and goosebumps broke out on Ellie's skin. Her gaze skipped over a wall of professional-grade tools. To her surprise, there was a section of guns. It was tempting to snag one, but with Owen in her arms, she had no way to do so.

Escape had to be carefully calculated. Right now, she didn't know who was outside or why the house was being attacked. She did trust that Mike wanted to live. Her best option was to stick with him.

"We'll take the Jeep." Mike seized Ellie's arm. His grip was bruising and his stare deadly as he shoved a handgun under her throat. "Get in and don't cause any trouble for me, or I'll make sure you regret it. Do we understand each other?"

"We do."

He released her with a shove. Ellie stumbled into the guard behind her, who already had the rear door open and waiting. She tightened her hold on little Owen, and using the running board, lifted herself into the back. "There's no car seat."

Mike shoved a key into the ignition. "Are you serious right now?"

She was actually. They were about to tear through explosions and gunfire. Ellie had no intention of doing so with an unsecured baby in the back seat.

She laid Owen down on the bench. His skin was sweaty after being pressed up against her for so long. Her heart stuttered. Or maybe it was the fever returning? He was supposed to be on antibiotics and surely had missed his last dose. The thought sent a fresh wave of panic through her, but with the more immediate threats on their doorstep, she shoved her worry to the side. She needed to figure out a way to securely strap in Owen.

The guard loomed over her, one foot on the running board as he hefted himself into the Jeep.

Gunshots erupted in the cavernous space. Ellie threw herself on top of Owen as the guard clutched his chest and then dropped away from the door. Through the strands of her dirty and smoke-filled hair, she registered two things at once. Daniel. He stood in the garage next to the wall of tools. Blood soaked his pants leg, and he looked unsteady on his feet, but it didn't affect the way he wielded the handgun. And Mike. The criminal was already shifting into position to fire at Daniel.

"NO!" Ellie launched herself over the rear seat and attacked Mike from behind, knocking the arm holding the gun upward with one hand as she scratched at his face with the other. Her nail jabbed his eye, and he howled like a wounded animal. Footsteps pounded over the cement.

"El! Release him!"

She immediately heeded Daniel's command, and he yanked Mike from the vehicle before delivering a stunning blow to the other man's head. Mike slumped to the floor, unconscious. Ellie climbed out of the Jeep just as the injured guard bolted for the garage exit.

She threw her arms around Daniel, nearly toppling him over. He caught himself on the door of the Jeep, wrapping his arms around her and planting a toe-curling kiss on her mouth.

"I thought you were dead." Tears threatened to

stream down her face, but she battled them back. Gunshots in the house brought the reality of their situation crashing down. They weren't out of trouble yet. "We have to get out of here."

She quickly bent down and retrieved Tyler's phone from Mike's pocket, handing it to Daniel, before pocketing the flash drive.

"Get in," Daniel ordered. "I'll drive."

"I'll drive. You can barely see." Ellie quickly undid her belt and pulled it from her waist. "Owen's in the back. Get in there with him. Second bench seat."

To her relief, Daniel didn't argue. Maybe he realized how close he was to passing out. He cradled Owen in his strong arms as Ellie quickly used her belt to secure the baby to Daniel's seat belt, similar to how a child under the age of two was secured in an airplane. Daniel grinned at her, his busted lip painfully swollen. "Smart."

"It'll hold in an accident. Let's pray we won't need it."

She stole one more kiss from Daniel and ran her hand over Owen's sweet curls before jumping into the driver's seat. She pressed the biggest button on the built-in visor and was relieved when the garage door in front of them rumbled open.

And then she got a look at the world outside.

Fire and smoke poured from the woods and into the house. Gunfire erupted from the front lawn as men in camo raced toward the burning inferno. They were caught in a turf war. Momentary panic stole Ellie's breath as she realized the gravel drive she'd taken to get here was blocked. The estate was an unknown to her. "I don't know where to go."

"There's a road to the north," Daniel said. "I used it to approach the house. It'll mean going off-road, but the Jeep can handle it."

Ellie shoved the vehicle into Drive and hit the gas. "Hang on!"

The Jeep shot out of the garage. Stones spun as she whipped around the corner with the skill of a race car driver. Muzzles flashed as men began firing at them. Ellie ducked, pressing harder on the gas, and then realization dawned. None of the windows were shattering.

The Jeep had bulletproof glass.

She raced toward the north side of the property as men scattered to get out of the vehicle's way. More gunfire followed. The path ahead was clear for exactly thirty seconds. Then she saw the roadblock. A wall of flames spreading rapidly across the grounds, the inferno fed by wind that pushed it hungrily toward the house. The blazing barrier was too wide to circumvent.

They had to go through it.

Ellie gritted her teeth and gripped the steering wheel. "Daniel, hang on tight to our boy."

TWENTY-EIGHT

Daniel opened his eye and groaned. Every single part of his body ached, including muscles he hadn't known existed. The scent of antiseptic and, strangely, warm apples hit his nose. Machines beeped. He fumbled with the device attached to the hospital bed, hitting the button that would move him into a sitting position.

"Morning, sunshine." Jonah sat in the chair next to the bed, his feet propped up on the railing. He winced. "Oof. I didn't think it was possible to make you look any uglier, but those guys managed."

He grunted in reply. "El..." It hurt to talk.

"She's with Owen. He's fine, but the doctors admitted him for monitoring since he missed so many doses of his antibiotics."

Daniel vaguely remembered a conversation with her about that, but he'd been swimming in pain medication at that point and not quite with it. Jonah dropped his feet, poured water into a cup, and helped bring the straw to Daniel's mouth. The cool liquid eased the ache in his vocal cords and instantly made him feel better. He held the cup on his own and drank more.

Jonah stretched his neck. His clothes were rumpled, and he desperately needed a shave. "I'll pretend my feelings aren't hurt that you immediately ask for Ellie, although I've been camped out next to your bed all night." His palms landed on the railing. "But deep down, I am. Hurt, I mean."

Daniel chuckled and instantly groaned. "Shut up. Do not make me laugh." He drank more water and, as the fatigue and drowsiness faded, his strength returned. Along with hunger. His nose lifted. "What's that smell?"

"It's you, man. You haven't showered in two days."

Daniel laughed again. The pain was less intense this time, but it still hurt. "I'm gonna hit the call button and make the nurse throw you out if you don't stop cracking jokes."

Jonah grinned. "I'd like you to go ahead and try it, old man."

"Watch who you're calling old. There are some grays in your beard."

He self-consciously rubbed a hand over the scruff on his face. "You turn thirty-seven and it all goes downhill." Jonah reached for a bakery box on the nightstand. "Homemade apple fritters, courtesy of your mom."

Daniel spent the next few hours pulling himself together. After eating, he took a shower, and with Jonah's help, put on sweatpants and a T-shirt. The nurse offered more pain meds, but he refused them. They made him groggy. His face was a mass of bruises, but his nose wasn't broken and he still had all his teeth. He considered that a win.

During the process of getting ready, Jonah filled him in on everything that'd occurred with the case. Every member of the Iron Fist, along with Tobias's crew, had been captured, effectively destroying both groups. It'd helped that many of the gang members were at Mike's house, shooting it out with one another. The rangers, along with the state tactical team, swept in and arrested anyone who wasn't already dead. Gideon Voss was pulled from a fancy dinner party and slapped in handcuffs.

Lena's evidence ensured none of them would ever see the light of day again.

"Mike began working for the Iron Fist about eight years ago." Jonah handed Daniel a comb. "At first, he used the money to pay down his debts, but as time went on, he fed more and more information in order to amass more power. We suspect he's the one who told Gideon about Lena and Ellie's plan, which led to the warehouse shooting. Mike and Gideon both thought that was the end of it."

"Until Lena's letter showed up at the FBI office."

He nodded. "By then, Mike had learned that Ellie survived the shooting, but he didn't know her new name or her location. They spent the next three years trying to find her. Meanwhile, Tobias broke away from the group and started a turf war. He spotted Ellie in the social media post and made a plan to use her to get ahold of the evidence. Spies in his camp working for Gideon shared the news and suddenly Ellie was being attacked from all angles."

Daniel gingerly combed his hair. "So the news that Tobias was dead turned out to be fake?"

"Yes. There was an attempt on his life, and the Iron Fist genuinely thought he was dead, but he'd merely gone underground to plan a new attack. The one he carried out at Mike's house." Jonah leaned against the bed. "Now Tobias will spend the rest of his life in prison, along with the rest of them. The evidence Lena collected included a few other law enforcement officers who were acting as moles for the Iron Fist, as well as some politicians that were also on the payroll. Every one of them is going down. It's over."

Relief uncoiled the last knot in Daniel's stomach. Ellie and Owen were safe. Finally. He set the comb down on the tray table. "You know what I can't understand. How would Mike have explained things to law enforcement when they stormed the house looking for me and Ellie?"

"Well, it turns out the property is registered as a private security training facility, complete with fake permits and everything. Mike intended for you and Ellie to be long gone by the time backup arrived, so once they searched the property and confirmed you weren't there—"

"There would be nothing they could do." Daniel

shook his head. It was terrifying to think how differently things could have turned out. The relief he'd felt moments ago doubled, knowing how close they'd all come to disaster. "What's Owen's room number?"

"I'll walk you there."

"I don't need an escort. I'm up and moving just fine." Daniel had taken a beating, and needed a few days to recover, but he was feeling much more like his old self. It would take time for the bruises to heal, but he'd survive. And maybe he was a bit prideful as well. Ellie had seen him weak as a newborn baby and pumped up on pain meds. He wanted her to know he was fine, a message that would be diminished by Jonah's handholding. "Thanks for everything, but you look exhausted. Go home. Get some rest."

Jonah shook his head. "Can't do it. Your mom put me under strict orders to make sure you don't face-plant trying to be macho." He pushed off the bed. "I'll walk you to Owen's room but won't go inside. That way Ellie can see you powering on your own steam."

Daniel rolled his eyes. "I'm not being macho. And it's more than a little irritating that you can read my mind."

"You're a man in love. Ain't no secret to how a guy thinks when he's trying to impress a woman."

Jonah's cell phone rang. Daniel saw the name flashing on the screen and snagged the device from the tray table. He hit speaker to answer the call. "Laney, Jonah is driving me insane. Can you do something with him?"

A rich, throaty laugh filled the room. "Want me to arrest him? I do have law enforcement authority now."

"In a state forest," Jonah retorted. "What's your jurisdiction? A few thousand acres of trees? That's not the flex you think it is, Laney." He glowered. "And don't you dare take Daniel's side. He's refusing to let me escort him across the hospital while recovering from a busted-open gunshot wound, a beating, and three broken ribs."

"He's kinda gotcha there, Daniel. And Jonah, I'm not taking sides. I'm Switzerland, neutral."

Jonah jabbed a finger in his chest. "You're my best friend. By contract, you have to always take my side. Why do I need to explain that?"

"Okay, I can see tensions are running high this morning. Have you had your coffee?"

"No," he muttered.

"Get some coffee and then call me back." Laney chuckled. "You'll be in a better mood."

"I don't need you to tell me what to do."

"Now who's being obstinate?" she shot back.

Daniel grinned. "She's got you there."

Jonah ripped the phone out of Daniel's hand. "Call you later, Laney. Stay out of trouble."

"Never. Bye, Daniel. Glad you're okay."

"Thanks."

Jonah hung up and tucked the phone into his back pocket. "I don't like the two of you teaming up against me."

Daniel laughed and then eyed his friend speculatively as they stepped into the hallway. "How come you and Laney never dated? It's obvious the two of you are good for each other."

"We tried once. Complete disaster. We work as friends." Jonah scowled. "You're not going to turn into one of those sappy guys now, are you? The kind that continuously try to set their friends up now that they're in a committed relationship."

"Is that what I'm in?" Daniel was overjoyed at the thought.

"Man, you are so far in, I can hear wedding bells."

Me too. But Daniel didn't want to share that thought yet. The first person he wanted to bare his heart to was Ellie. His steps picked up as excitement at seeing her and Owen sank into him. A short elevator ride and a few turns down the corridor later, he was standing in front of a hospital room in the pediatric department. He planted his palm on the cracked-open door and glanced back at Jonah. "Thanks."

His friend grinned. "Just remember all my good deeds when it comes time to pick a best man."

Daniel laughed and shook his head before pushing the door open and stepping into the room. The murmur of their voices registered first. Owen's babble punctuated by Ellie's lilting tones as she read a book to him. He paused, just a moment, and lifted his attention toward the ceiling. *Thank you, God.*

A simple prayer, but a heartfelt one. Daniel rounded the curtain separating the bed from the door, his gaze drinking in the sight before him. Ellie was sitting on an armchair, a train book in one hand, her other arm wrapped around Owen, who was in her lap. Her hair shimmered in the sunshine pouring in through the window and her face was makeup free. She appeared tired but content. Owen played with Scout's ear as he leaned into his mother's embrace. His cheeks were rosy with good health, and he babbled constantly.

Daniel felt it. His heart tumbling over and over again.

And just when he thought his chest was close to bursting with love, Ellie glanced up. Her smile was radiant and warm, melting away every ache in his battered body, and the warmth in her eyes... it stole his breath.

"You're up!" Ellie lowered the book. "Why didn't Jonah call me?"

She started to rise, but he waved her back down. Crossing the room, he bent at the waist to place a gentle kiss on her lips. Owen grinned adorably and lifted his arms in a silent invitation for Daniel to hold him. Ellie's eyes widened. "You have a super fan. He almost never wants anyone else to hold him when I'm reading a story."

Daniel wasn't about to turn down Owen's offer. He started to lift him, but his broken ribs screamed in protest, and he winced. Ellie immediately stood, bringing Owen with her. "Sit, sweetheart. He can sit on your lap, if that won't hurt too much."

"I'll be fine." Daniel settled into the armchair, and Ellie gingerly placed Owen in the crook of his arm. The little boy smelled like baby powder and soap and that magical scent only babies had. Daniel cuddled him close, ignoring the ache in his side from his ribs, and kissed

Owen's head. A sense of rightness settled over him. He didn't know how or when, but somehow Owen had become a part of him.

He glanced up at Ellie. "It looks like he's feeling better."

"Much better. His fever broke this morning, so he's on the mend, unless a new complication arises." She brushed a gentle touch across a bruise on his cheek. "What about you? The doctors were worried about head trauma. You had a concussion."

That explained the nausea that nearly had him tossing his cookies while trying to save Ellie and Owen. Daniel took her fingers and kissed the soft curve of her palm. "Don't worry. I'm fine." His gaze swept over her, cataloging all the details. The scratch marring her cheek, the softness of her lips and the faint circles under her eyes. His mind flashed back to the harrowing moment their Jeep flew through the flames. It'd been terrifying to see the blaze approaching the windshield, knowing there was nothing he could do to protect her if the fire broke through their car.

Daniel shoved the thought away. Ellie had driven like a pro and their escape, while treacherous, had been a success. They were all here now, safe and sound. "Have you slept at all in the last two days?"

"Some."

Likely very little. She was running on fumes. Somehow, he was going to have to convince her to go back to the ranch to rest but doubted that would happen as long as Owen was in the hospital. She wouldn't leave him, not even in the trusting care of his mother.

The door to the room swung open, and Maggie Lyons, the social worker, bustled in. Her eyes widened as she registered their presence, and a frown instantly formed on her lips. "What are you two doing in here? Owen's supposed to be with his foster parents."

TWENTY-NINE

Daniel watched Ellie's face drain of color as the bottom dropped out of her world. In all the craziness, she'd clearly forgotten that she'd been removed as Owen's foster mother. Her fingers trembled as she placed a protective hand on Owen. "His foster parents never showed up to the hospital. I don't know if they were notified or if they were too scared after what happened. I've been with him the whole time."

Maggie's frown deepened as she set her briefcase on the tray table. "That's something I'll have to look into. Foster parents can't simply shirk their responsibilities. Owen's kidnapping scared them, understandably, but they should've contacted my office and said that they weren't ready to step back into caring for him." She planted her hands on her hips. "What is it about foster parents refusing to call my office?"

"Maybe they're worried about what you'll say," Daniel drawled, a hint of anger coloring his voice. This woman had taken Owen away from Ellie, and while a part of him understood she was just following orders, another part of him blamed Maggie for the ordeal Owen had been through.

Maggie sniffed. "I suppose you think I owe you an apology."

"Not me, ma'am. Ellie, however, most certainly. She didn't do anything wrong. She protected Owen with her life, and might I add, warned you that removing him from the ranch would put him in greater danger. Turned out she was right." His tone turned harder with every word. "Owen was kidnapped less than twenty-four hours after you removed him from Ellie's care. And the only reason he's here now is because she put her life at risk to rescue him. So yep, she deserves every apology you can give, and I still don't think it'll be enough."

"Daniel..." Ellie placed a hand on his shoulder. The move was meant to calm his anger, and it did, but he didn't regret sticking up for her. Not now. Not ever.

Taking care of her and Owen was a blessing he willingly accepted.

As if to punctuate that thought, little Owen stuck his thumb in his mouth and leaned against Daniel, hugging Scout close. His eyelids were growing heavy. The trust this child so freely gave him... it melted his heart.

Maggie sighed. "You're right, Ranger Perez." She shifted her attention to Ellie. "I could try to defend myself by saying that I was just following orders, but the truth is, that's no justification. I'm Owen's social worker.

The responsibility lies with me, and I could've fought harder to keep him with you. I'm sorry."

Ellie shook her head. "No. I put you in a terrible position by lying about my identity to you and the court. I'm sorry for misleading you. It was never designed to break your trust, although I completely understand that it did."

"About that..." Maggie popped open her briefcase. "The emergency hearing regarding Owen's removal from your home was held this morning."

Ellie inhaled sharply, and Daniel felt his temper spark once more. He didn't yell in deference to Owen, who was quickly dropping off to sleep, but his words were edged with steel when he said, "You didn't think that was something Ellie should know about?"

"I sent a text and an email."

Ellie's complexion was ghostly pale as she lifted a hand to her mouth. "I don't have my cell phone. It's still back at the ranch. In all the confusion..." Moisture shimmered in her gorgeous eyes. "Mrs. Lyons, please, can we have another hearing? I want to explain myself to the judge. I know it's a long shot, but—"

"There's no need." She perched a set of reading glasses on her nose. "A group of current and former FBI agents, including Special Agent in Charge Vincent Maddox and retired Special Agent in Charge James Callahan, testified in front of the judge. They were accompanied by a large contingent of Texas Rangers, who also testified. Every single one of them agreed that Owen should be returned to your care immediately."

Ellie seemed frozen in place, as if she was uncertain

she'd heard Maggie correctly. Daniel reached up to take her hand. He shook it gently. "Did you hear her, sweetheart? The judge gave Owen back to you."

The tears shimmering in her eyes spilled over her cheeks. She crouched down next to the chair and kissed Owen, before burying her face in Daniel's chest. "He's coming home with me. That's what she said, right?"

"Yes, El." Daniel wrapped an arm around her trembling form, his heart cracking wide open as her tears wet his shirt. "He's coming home with you."

She sucked in a breath and seemed to gather her runaway emotions under control before standing to face Maggie again. The older woman was watching them over the rim of her eyeglasses, and if Daniel wasn't mistaken, moisture glistened in her eyes too. She sniffed again and squared her shoulders. "I need you to sign some documents."

"Gladly." Ellie moved forward, reaching for the pen.

"What will you do about your name now that it's public knowledge you're Elizabeth Conway?"

Ellie paused, her pen above the paper. "I'm not Elizabeth Conway. Not anymore. I wondered for a while if I'd buried that part of myself when I went into hiding, but after all of this, I realize it was leaving things undone that truly bothered me. Now that the Iron Fist is dismantled, I'm free to choose who I want to be, and my real life began when I became Ellie Brooks. I have a community in Silver Creek, and I have Owen."

Maggie nodded. "Now, I want to be clear, your adoption application is still pending. The judge will have questions about lying to the court about your identity, and he may still ask the District Attorney to pursue charges of perjury, but SAC Maddox and SAC Callahan testified adamantly that you were following orders. It's my hope the judge will let it go, but that's not my call." She smiled gently. "You have good friends." Her gaze skipped to Daniel. "Both of you."

"Yes, we do." Ellie finished signing the paper with a flourish. "Thank you, Mrs. Lyons."

"No, Miss Brooks, I should be thanking you. You and Ranger Perez saved Owen's life." She clicked her briefcase closed. "I'll do everything I can to convince the judge that you deserve to adopt Owen. I may have to get in line to do it..." She chuckled. "But you can count on me being in your corner."

Her heels clipped against the tile as she left the room. Ellie turned to face Daniel, a stunned expression on her face. "Pinch me. I'm not sure I believe that just happened."

"Believe it, sweetheart." Daniel smiled, his heart filled with joy for her. Ellie was an amazing mother, and Owen was very blessed to have her. "When we're all released from the hospital, we should have a party at the ranch to celebrate. A justice-was-served-all-is-right-with-the-world party."

She laughed, the sound melodic and full of relief. "That might be hard to spell out with balloons." Her gaze softened as she took in Owen, completely asleep in Daniel's arms. "You two are absolutely precious together. I wish I had my cell phone so I could snap a photo."

The comment made Daniel's breath catch. It was something a woman might say about her husband and child. He'd vowed to give it some time, let them settle into life without danger stalking every move, but after nearly escaping death, it seemed ridiculous to put off saying what was in his heart. He started to rise from the chair, but Ellie drew closer.

"Here, let me take Owen first." She gently lifted the sleeping boy, and ever so carefully, laid him in the crib before covering him with a soft blanket.

Daniel joined her, wrapping an arm around her waist. An easy touch. Natural. As if he'd been doing it his whole life. Ellie leaned into him, resting her head on his shoulder, as they both watched Owen sleep. The baby's breathing was deep and regular, a small smile playing on his lips. And yet, even in slumber, he kept a solid grip on his favorite stuffed dog. Daniel smoothed a curl away from his cheek. "How does he manage to hold on to Scout like that, even in his sleep?"

Ellie chuckled. "I have no idea. You know I bought two extra Scouts and hid them in my bedroom closet. If we ever lose one, I wanted to have backups."

"Just one more reason you're such an amazing mom."

A cloud crossed her face. "Let's hope the judge thinks so too."

"He will." Daniel's heart picked up speed as a sudden case of nerves churned his stomach. "El... what would you think about modifying your adoption petition?"

Her brow furrowed as she lifted her head from his

shoulder and twisted to face him. "What do you mean? Like adding my real name—"

"No." He swallowed hard. "I want to marry you, and I'd like us to adopt Owen together. I love you both. So much it almost hurts sometimes. And I know it's fast. I probably should've waited until I had a ring picked out, taken you someplace special..." Daniel was just realizing how foolish this was. He'd proposed in the hospital next to Owen's bedside while his face and body were covered in bruises. He wasn't even sure he could get down on one knee without tearing his stitches out again. This was all wrong.

Judging by Ellie's shocked expression and stony silence, she agreed.

"I'm sorry. This wasn't well thought out. My mom put this ridiculous notion in my head. She and my dad married after two weeks and had a wonderful forty-five years together." Daniel shook his head. "We can take all the time you need. I'm not going anywhere. I just... wanted you to know what was in my heart."

She blinked. "You want to marry me?"

He nodded.

"And adopt Owen?"

Daniel nodded again. "But I don't want you to feel pressured. There's no rush—"

"Stop talking." For the second time, tears spilled down Ellie's cheeks. She stepped into the circle of his embrace, cupping his face with her delicate hands. "My answer is yes. Yes. A thousand times, yes."

Relief and joy crashed over him like a tidal wave. For

a moment, he couldn't speak, couldn't breathe, couldn't do anything but stare into her eyes and wonder how he'd gotten so lucky. This woman—this incredible, brave, beautiful woman—wanted to spend her life with him. Wanted to build a family with him.

"I love you, Daniel Perez, and I don't need a ring or fancy proposals or grand gestures. I want you. Someone who will fight to make our relationship work, who loves me deeply. Quiet and steady, a good friend, and a caring family man. Someone who will help me raise Owen with strong values and a deep faith." Her thumbs brushed against the bruises on his cheeks. "I prayed for someone like you, and I'm so grateful God brought us together."

Daniel couldn't wait another second. He lowered his head and captured her lips with his, pouring every ounce of love, gratitude, and promise into the kiss. It was tender and sweet. Reverent, but passionate enough to heat his blood. It was a kiss full of promises—of forever, of family, of a love that had been tested by fire and emerged stronger than steel.

Ellie melted into him, her hands sliding from his cheeks to wind around his neck, and for a moment, the rest of the world simply disappeared. There was only their love and the future stretching out before them like a beautiful dream finally coming true.

When they finally parted, Daniel's joy couldn't be measured as Ellie laid her head on his chest. They stood there for a long time, just holding each other and relishing the moment. Then he gently brushed her hair away from her temple and tucked it behind her ear.

"What do you think about telling everyone about our engagement? We could turn the justice-was-served-all-is-right-with-the-world party into an engagement announcement."

"Actually, I have a better idea. What do you think about making it a wedding reception?"

Texas Ranger Heroes Series

Ranger Protection

Ranger Redemption

Ranger Courage

Ranger Faith

Ranger Honor

Ranger Justice

Ranger Integrity

Ranger Loyalty

Ranger Bravery

Triumph Over Adversity Series

Calculated Risk

Critical Error

Necessary Peril

Strategic Plan

Covert Mission

Tactical Force

Would you like to know when my next book is released? Or when my novels go on sale? It's easy. Subscribe to my newsletter at www.lynnshannon.com and all of the info will come straight to your inbox!

Reviews help readers find books. Please consider leaving a review at your favorite place of purchase or anywhere you discover new books. Thank you.

9 781953 244635